THE
HAGGI
CONNECTION

An engrossing and amusing debut adventure
featuring the mysterious Haggi warriors

By

Stephen Easingwood

Copyright © STEPHEN EASINGWOOD 2024
This book is sold subject to the condition that it shall not, by way of trade or otherwise, be lent, resold, hired out, or otherwise circulated without the publisher's prior consent in any form of binding or cover other than that in which it is published and without a similar condition including this condition being imposed on the subsequent publisher.
The moral right of STEPHEN EASINGWOOD has been asserted.
ISBN: 9798880358038

This is a work of fiction. Names, characters, businesses, organizations, places, events and incidents either are the product of the author's imagination or are used fictitiously. Any resemblance to actual persons, living or dead, events, or locales is entirely coincidental.

CONTENTS

PROLOGUE 1
CHAPTER 1 4
CHAPTER 2 12
CHAPTER 3 17
CHAPTER 4 23
CHAPTER 5 31
CHAPTER 6 36
CHAPTER 7 43
CHAPTER 8 47
CHAPTER 9 54
CHAPTER 10 63
CHAPTER 11 71
CHAPTER 12 75
CHAPTER 13 79
CHAPTER 14 85
CHAPTER 15 89
CHAPTER 16 93
CHAPTER 17 99
CHAPTER 18 105
CHAPTER 19 112
CHAPTER 20 114
CHAPTER 21 126
CHAPTER 22 130
CHAPTER 23 136
CHAPTER 24 144
CHAPTER 25 149
CHAPTER 26 152
CHAPTER 27 158
CHAPTER 28 167
CHAPTER 29 174
CHAPTER 30 179
CHAPTER 31 184
CHAPTER 32 187
CHAPTER 33 195
CHAPTER 34 197
CHAPTER 35 200
CHAPTER 36 208

CHAPTER 37	212
CHAPTER 38	218
CHAPTER 39	227
CHAPTER 40	231
EPILOGUE	235
JOCKANESE TRANSLATOR	240

I hope you enjoy reading this book as much as I enjoyed writing it.

If this book doesn't stir your imagination and emotions then I've not done my job properly.

I honestly burst out laughing at some of the Haggi banter and antics as I was writing it and the last page of the Epilogue gets to me every single time I read it. Have fun.

Stephen Easingwood

Prologue

2002, somewhere in central Scotland

Hamish McPherson was a quiet, skilled and moderately successful artist in his mid-forties. He had a feeling he was safe, and among friends, but couldn't be sure.

The artist was growing increasingly weary of the blindfold he'd been wearing for a good twenty minutes. He wasn't restrained in any way but was lying flat on his back and felt like he was being carried along on a metal tray.

It was strangely quiet all around him but an occasional bump of his transport made him moan slightly.

"Nae much further, chief," said the first voice Hamish had heard since before his blindfold had gone on.

Two minutes later, there was a noticeable cooling of the air and Hamish was helped upright and placed on a comfortable chair. His blindfold was removed and he struggled to adjust his eyes to the new light around him.

He was in a large, bright, dome-shaped room with limited decoration, other than a few emblematic Scottish clan crests. Some additional colour was provided via the range of tartan clothing worn by his hosts. His seating place was in the open mouth of a horseshoe, made out of low-level tables.

Surrounding him were about a dozen strange-looking, hairy wee beings, all seated and looking eagerly up at him.

Now I understand how Gulliver felt, Hamish briefly thought, as he awaited the opening gambit.

One of the wee hairy beings, presumably the leader, stood up.

He didn't get much taller, if at all.

Through his Highland heritage and the knowledge of his mother and grandmother, Hamish knew a fair bit about the many Scottish clans. The distinct, predominantly yellow tartan-patterned plaid and the prominent golden sun emblem on the sporran buckle pointing at him, indicated a connection to the MacLeod clan of Lewis.

The presumed MacLeod didn't give his name or clan but he did speak. "Hamish, welcome tae oor Senior Council 'n' apologies fir the blindfold 'n' uncomfy journey. A necessary evil tae protect oor location, which Ah'm sure ye understand. Ah'll nae beat aboot the bush. Yir here so we kin reward ye fir yer ootstandin' help 'n' service in protecting oor habitat 'n' lifestyle."

He went all posh at that point and, in proper English, continued, "You're probably not even aware of your vital actions on our behalf but without your efforts, we might no longer exist in our heartland. Accordingly, we wish to reward you with our medal of honour. In addition, we forever stand at the disposal of you and yours, should you require our help in future."

Hamish was then handed a small box with a felt-like cover, which didn't have much weight to it.

The artist opened the box and saw, not so much a medal, but a kaleidoscope of coloured light, coming from a clear, glass-like base, in the shape of a capital H. Hamish thought it was the most beautiful thing he'd ever seen and simply said, "Thank you, I'm honoured."

Offers of food and drink followed. The last thing Hamish remembered before falling into a very sound sleep, was hearing something to do with mixing berries and water in a secret recipe.

With no idea how long had passed, Hamish awoke with a grunt. He found himself in bright daylight and seated in his comfy old armchair in the cottage he lived in with his wife, Isabella. He was sweating heavily and had a fuzzy head as he slowly pieced together what seemed like a bizarre dream.

Blindfolded... lying on my back... furry wee creatures that talk... MacLeod tartan... a beautiful light... a promise of help... berries...? What a load of nonsense!

He rubbed his bloodshot eyes and stretched his arms upwards to free up his aching back muscles. As he did so he glanced to his right and there, on his side table, was a felt-covered box.

As Hamish opened the box, he was met by a mini Northern Lights display and a quiet voice said, "Help from the hill is yours, always."

My god, it wasn't a dream.

Chapter 1

around 20 years later,

after Covid restrictions

Scotland, on a crisp, bright, Saturday in March.

The thin blanket of white frost was just about off the grass, the sunlight and warming morning air doing their work.

A few weeks short of turning eleven, Duncan McPherson sat distractedly at his bedroom window, contemplating with chin on hands. His gaze was in the direction of the heavily forested hills in the middle distance. Picking up his hand-me-down binoculars from the window ledge, Duncan zoomed in more closely.

On Huntsmen Hill overlooking the town, the smoke from the chimney of the old shepherd's bothy was, unusually, going straight up.

Thankfully no school today and good weather means I'll get out and about – YEESSS.

He'd been up for a while and eaten cereal (*good old Coco Pops*) for breakfast, with his mum Cath and big sister Mary for company. Young Duncan had eaten his cereal in comparative quiet, passed pleasantries with the two main female presences in his life, then retreated to the haven of his bedroom.

Into his own safe little world.

From his bedroom window Duncan could hear distinct shouts of young football players. These shouts were supplemented by calls from heavily invested parents, plus the occasional shrill blast of the referee's whistle coming from the nearby sports pitches. One such shrill whistle blast set off a shrieking scream in Duncan's head, for which he had no explanation. He covered his ears and recoiled under the covers of his bed, to try to block out that horrible noise.

Football, a major deal to many in Scotland, was definitely not his thing, nor was any other sport for that matter. Duncan hated loud noise and crowds of people, preferring quiet places, nature, and largely his own company.

His dad George had left last year to take up with another woman; 'The Bitch', as his mother called her. Although he didn't see his dad much since the break-up, there was one big upside. The tedious, father/son football kick-around sessions, which his dad loved, were no longer imposed on the physically uncoordinated Duncan.

His best and only real friend, Davy Smith, was another quiet and non-mainstream soul so they were tight, like bonded brothers. They would normally spend time together at weekends or after school, wandering around the countryside and keeping out of the way of others. This was easy to do in Auchterbarn, a lovely rural spot in central Scotland. There were multiple walks and open-air adventures galore within minutes from their homes.

One of Duncan's favourite haunts was down by the nearby burn, where he could watch and listen to the ever-changing water for hours. There was also time and space to look for birds and other creatures that frequented the fields and the banks of the burn, as it made its way through the landscape.

Duncan used his grandad's binoculars regularly and often took them on his field trips. He also had a tiny fishing rod, which he took along on some water visits, but it was more a prop than anything else.

The fact I've never caught a fish might be a bit of a giveaway.

His pal Davy Smith was away 'through the West' with his family this weekend, so wasn't around, although Duncan desperately needed a breakout from his room.

He bounced up from his vantage point, grabbed his hoodie off the peg on the back of the door, then slipped on his unfashionable, well-broken-in trainers. Instinctively, he gathered up his sketch pad and put some pencils in his pocket as he bumbled downstairs, seeking open air.

Mary, his big sister, looked up and said, "Oh, so the spectre has left his room. Where are you off to? Davy's away this weekend."

"I'm going up to the graveyard to check on Grandad," retorted Duncan.

"God knows why you go up there so often, it's soooo boring. What do you do?"

"Just sketch stuff and chat to Grandad."

"Why?"

"Just… because I want to… and it makes me feel better."

Mum Cath broke up the sibling squabble by saying, "It's fine, Duncan, just ignore Mary, so long as you like it. Just remember to stay safe and be back here for lunch around one. Have you got your watch on?"

"Yip," was Duncan's in-depth response.

Duncan loped awkwardly towards the front door, his long legs and sizeable feet seemingly too big for his young body. He flicked his lengthy, untidy hair out of his eyes, as he quickly looked back over his shoulder and stuck his tongue out at his big sister.

His rare act of defiance felt good.

It was dry outside so there were no puddles to avoid but Duncan made a big effort not to step on any pavement cracks, skipping across the joints to avoid getting any 'bad luck'. As he reached the turning into the church road, he tried to put his annoying sister out of his mind.

Although he was a fair bit taller than her, Mary was just under two years older than Duncan. She could be mouthy and VERY annoying to her wee brother but, to be fair, she didn't ignore him completely, which many others did. Mary was clever, pretty, cool and popular, which made him feel fairly envious when compared to what he thought he had to offer.

On reaching the old church graveyard, he switched his focus away from his sibling.

There was one older man tending his wife's grave but Duncan was too shy and self-conscious to speak to him. The old man seemed vaguely familiar. He might have been a friend of his grandad, although Duncan wasn't sure.

He wandered round the sunlight-free, north-facing corner, passed the church and turned into the adjoining graveyard. The trees threw shadows across the sunlit graves and a light breeze gently rustled some long fallen leaves.

Duncan walked slowly and respectfully, with his head

bowed, along the paths to the familiar, far corner of the cemetery.

He stood stock still as he looked intently at his grandparents' gravestone, noticing the fresh yellow daffodils on display. His eyes moistened a little, like they always did, as he read their names, the words and the dates. Taking in every detail, inscribed in gold leaf on the dark granite headstone, even though these were already ingrained in his brain.

He hadn't really known his dad's mum, Granny Bella, as she passed away when he was very young, as had his maternal grandparents. Grandad Hamish, however, had only left them fairly recently, shortly after their dad George had left them in a very different way.

Duncan had never spent a great deal of time alone with his Grandad Hamish but always felt strangely comfortable around him. This was odd as almost everyone else made Duncan uneasy.

In addition, they had their own wee 'pull ma finger' ritual.

Whenever Grandad needed to fart, *which was fairly often*, he would point his 'trigger' finger towards Duncan, make a clicking noise as if cocking a trigger, and say, "Pull ma finger, son." Duncan's finger pull would thus trigger Hamish's gas release.

This was their wee secret thing and Duncan quietly smiled as he thought about it.

"Hi, Grandad Hamish, hope everything's good with you," Duncan whispered, self-consciously, in the direction of the grave. He then moved over to the nearby wooden bench, opened up his sketch pad and dug a pencil out of the pocket of his very much non-designer jeans.

Once he settled, Duncan's pencil started to move fluently

over the paper, as he skilfully sketched a picture of the scene in front of him.

He lost himself in his artistic craft.

Ten minutes later, out of the corner of his eye, he noticed the old man leave and Duncan relaxed as he then had the whole graveyard space to himself.

Another twenty minutes or so rolled by, by which time he was halfway through his sketch and lost in his own world.

Duncan suddenly jolted upright as he thought he'd heard a voice.

He stopped drawing and sat forward, listening more intently.

Faint words. "Come over here, son. I need to tell you something."

Duncan quickly swivelled round. Spooked. Scanning to check there was no one there or that he was being pranked. He couldn't see anything but was buzzing with adrenaline as the voice repeated, "Come over here, son. I need to tell you something IMPORTANT."

It was louder this time and sounded awfully like Grandad Hamish.

Duncan was a bit freaked out but slowly edged off the bench.

He tiptoed uneasily towards his grandparents' grave, swivelling, checking all around, half expecting someone to jump out from behind a grave.

As clear as day, Hamish's voice spoke to Duncan. It was as if he was standing right next to him.

"We didn't speak much while I was still with you, son. I thought I'd be around a lot longer than I was but there you go, never assume. You might not realise, but I know stuff. I'm still around and notice what goes on. The thing is, I have a big, no, a HUGE secret to tell you and I'm telling you now as I was too late in my lifetime. I knew your dad wasn't suited to what I'm passing on, but you have the right stuff, I've no doubt. You're a really good kid. You have special talents, like your drawing, but… because you're not like the other kids and don't fit in… you are misunderstood… get treated badly and bullied. That's just not right."

Duncan stood and stared into space, dumbfounded, open-mouthed at the words he was hearing. Words that were both seemingly from beyond this world, but also a bit too accurate for comfort.

Hamish's words continued. "Now, I know that you're not one to make a fuss or fight back but I want you to know that there is help available. It's just not like any help you've ever known. I've had access to this help for about twenty years and now I'm going to pass the details on to YOU. Hamish, you are going to be a CONNECTOR, with the ability to summon help from the hill. Oh NO, watch out… someone is coming just now… I'll give you more details later. You'll hear from me again soon son, I promise. Cheers for now."

No sooner had the last word been uttered than a plump woman, wearing a headscarf and winter coat, turned the corner into the graveyard. As his grandad's voice faded away, the woman said to an ashen-faced Duncan, "Nice day, laddie."

Duncan couldn't speak and felt like his feet were cemented into the ground.

With a huge effort, he freed his leaden feet, turned and ran from the graveyard at speed. He didn't dare to look back, his mind in a whirlwind and legs moving faster than he ever thought possible.

Once round the corner from the church, Duncan stopped,

pressed his back against the cold of the stone wall and urged himself... *slow down... and... breathe.*

After a couple of minutes, despite some strange looks from passengers in passing cars, Duncan felt calmer and his heart rate was nearer normal. While still in total shock at what had just happened, he felt a new, warm feeling of strength and hope.

His Grandad truly believed in him and he was going to have the chance to be a somebody – a CONNECTOR, whatever that was!

Chapter 2

With Duncan away to the graveyard and Mary round at her best pal Steph's house, Cath trudged wearily upstairs to start doing the weekly ironing. As she opened the cupboard to dig out the ironing kit, she caught sight of herself in the internal cupboard mirror.

Cath wasn't overly impressed with what reflected back at her.

This slightly tubby, medium-height woman, with sad green eyes and tied-back dirty blonde hair, was a far cry from the stunning bride she'd been on her wedding day, fourteen years before.

Fat, faithless and forty-ish, not a good combo, she thought to herself.

Cath pushed her negative thought away and dutifully lifted out the ironing board, pulling the cushioned top upwards. The ratchet creaked as the board stabilised and she settled the holder in the last groove.

Cath looked round onto the ottoman at the bottom of her bed, to check how much ironing needed to be done. She took one look at the huge mound of clothes, groaned frustratedly, and went straight back downstairs.

A few minutes later, she had a mug of steaming hot, sugared coffee wrapped in her hands. She felt her fingers warming as she gazed out of the kitchen window, contemplating how she'd arrived here.

Cath(erine) Mary Campbell, as she was then, had met husband George around eighteen years before. She was in her early twenties and out for a drink in Perth city centre with Helen, her friend and fellow student at college. They were in the second year of a three-year course in business administration.

While chatting attentively at their small table, a group of guys came into the pub. One of them accidentally stumbled and bumped into Cath's arm, which in turn knocked both the girls' drinks all over the floor.

The 'bumper' was, of course, George.

He was suitably embarrassed, apologised profusely and asked the girls what they would like as replacement drinks. Cath and Helen both smiled politely and asked for dry white wine, while they mopped up the soaked table top.

As George made his way to the bar for their wine, Cath gave him a sly once over. He was no heartthrob but was six-foot-plus, with legs that looked too long for his slim body, and had a short sensible haircut.

When he returned with the apology drinks, she noticed he also had nice teeth and a pleasant smile. He'd brought a pint along with the two glasses of wine.

They all introduced themselves and George chatted awkwardly to the girls for a few minutes, before returning to his mates. It turned out he was a bit older than the girls, originally from Perth and in the second half of a course in architecture at Glasgow University. He was home for the weekend, visiting family.

As George went back to his pals, the girls briefly swapped their thoughts on him, then returned to their drinks and the wider gossip of the day.

About twenty-five minutes later, George's group of pals finished up their drinks and headed out through a different door than they'd come in. George, however, came back to the table where the girls were still seated and said to Cath, "Sorry about earlier. I think you're really pretty and I'd like to do something more to make up for the drink spill. Can I have your phone number, please?"

She was a bit surprised and definitely not in the habit of giving out her number to people she hardly knew.

Eventually, with Helen's encouragement, Cath's uncertainty crumbled and she scribbled her student flat telephone number on a beer mat and handed it to George. A decision that would alter her life, although she didn't know it at the time.

George phoned Cath's flat a few days later and they agreed to meet up the following weekend for drinks and dinner in Perth city centre. Their first date went pretty well with no mishaps; Cath enjoyed herself and felt comfortable in George's company.

Things progressed slowly from there with only occasional get-togethers, due to the distance between their respective places of study.

George's mates considered that he was 'punching above his weight' with Cath. From her perspective, George wasn't what you'd call handsome or someone who made her heart sing. He was, however, much nicer than previous boyfriends and turned out to be a strong 'grower'.

By the time they completed their studies with good grades,

they were a loving and committed couple, well suited, with similar outlooks in life, music and the world in general. They tied the knot at a small church in Perth, around four years on from their first encounter. A modest gathering of family and friends were in attendance to share their big day.

It had been a lovely, sunny, happy day and Cath half smiled at the memory, before the reality of more recent events pushed into her mind.

Not long after the wedding they'd moved into a one-bed 'starter flat' in Perth. It was clear that they would like to have kids so they started married life with an agreed plan. The idea was for George to try to establish a reputation in the world of architecture as quickly as possible then, if it was viable, set up his own firm within five years. Cath would use her qualifications to find a 'solid' local job in the short term. Then, if everything went to plan, she'd give up work and put her energies into the maternal role she'd always secretly wished for.

Cath worked happily in an admin role for the local council for a couple of years and George was hugely successful, more quickly than they'd hoped. This was mainly due to a groundbreaking design that he won an award for, leading to him securing funding to start his own firm.

His company thrived and, when Cath fell pregnant with Mary, they had moved to the current family house in Auchterbarn, to (in Cath's mind) *live happily ever after.*

Mary was born a few months after they moved and Duncan followed almost two years later. Life was good, their family complete and they led a happy, settled and comfortable life in a lovely place, for over a decade.

Cath had no idea there were any bumps in the road until, a little over a year ago, George dropped the biggest of bombs.

"Cath, I'm sorry but I'm leaving, I've met someone else."

He packed a bag and left the house immediately to take up his new life with Marlene, his thirty-two-year-old mistress.

When Cath told the kids what had happened, Mary was devastated, whereas Duncan simply shrugged and went to his room.

Cath had cried herself into a soggy mess, racking her brain for what she'd done wrong. The answer was nothing at all but, initially, she couldn't stem the self-loathing and doubt pouring through her.

Through several months of hurt, Cath had kept things going for the kids and eventually got herself into a better place. She successfully gained a part-time job in the local medical practice, started going to a dance class with a female colleague from work, and just about reestablished her self-respect. Her anger now was angled on George and 'The Bitch' rather than on herself, which was progress of sorts.

George continued to be very successful as an architect and more than paid his way in child support. He made occasional contact and saw Mary and Duncan maybe every five or six weeks but he was no longer interested or invested in their family. The reality was that George was to all intents and purposes an absent, cash-machine father.

On this rather sobering thought, Cath jolted back to reality and realised she'd better start making lunch for Duncan coming back from his trip to the graveyard.

Chapter 3

Duncan gave himself a further few minutes to recompose after the revelations in the graveyard. He avoided any eye contact with passers-by, not wanting to betray his impending importance, as he made his way, slowly, back home.

After uneventfully passing various neighbouring houses, he reached number twenty-eight, went up the stairs and cautiously opened the front door. Bending down, Duncan untied his laces, took his trainers off, then started upstairs.

"Perfect timing, Dunc, lunch will be ready in five minutes," called his mum.

"A wee five minutes or a big five minutes?" he enquired.

"A wee five."

"OK, I'll not bother going upstairs. What's for lunch anyway?"

"Pie, beans and chips."

Simple but soooo good, maybe some ketchup... Perfect.

"Where's Mary?"

"She's away round to Steph's house so it's just you and me."

Even better, Little Miss Popular ain't here to give me a hard time.

About four minutes later, Cath took the pie and chips out of the oven and placed them carefully on Duncan's plate. She then added the steaming hot beans from the pan on the hob, taking care not to pour them on the pie or chips. Duncan didn't like that so best to stick to the usual routine.

"Looks fab, Mum, thanks. You not having any?"

"No, son, I'll maybe get a sandwich in a bit," Cath replied, with no real conviction. *I need to cut back on calorie intake after losing out to 'The Bitch'.*

Duncan started his standard eating method.

Ketchup, shake the bottle, add to chips.

Eat chips, one by one, till gone.

Beans, speared one at a time with his fork, quickly dispatched, till done.

Main event, the pie.

- ✓ Cut crust off the top of the pie, eat this first.
- ✓ Meat from the pie centre, munch and savour.
- ✓ Lastly, slowly finish off the pastry pie case.

Drink, orange diluting juice in a oner.

All done, loud burp. "Pardon."

Cath was intrigued, as always, but no longer surprised by her son's ritualistic eating habits.

His eating habits and general, reserved quietness remained unaltered, however, Cath had an inexplicable 'mother's instinct' that something within Duncan had changed. She felt a strong need to try to work out what that change might be. Her opening gambit was, "How did it go at the graveyard? Did you speak to anyone?"

Duncan nearly fell off his chair.

How could she know about Grandad Hamish, speaking from beyond the grave?

He regained his composure and simply said, "Fine, one older woman said hello but that was it."

"So what did you get up to then?"

"I read the gravestone, said hi to Grandad Hamish and Gran then sketched for a bit."

"OK, can I see your sketch, please?"

Duncan had never really shown anyone his artwork, as he didn't think it was any good or a big deal. As his mum had asked, he picked up his sketch pad from the chair, where he'd placed it on the way in, and handed it to her.

Cath opened the sketch pad and sat eyes wide and mouth open, aghast. She was looking at a partial drawing of the graveyard that could just as well be a PHOTOGRAPH. The detail was incredible, off the scale...

"Wow, Dunc, this drawing is absolutely awesome... I had no idea you could draw like this."

"Well you've never asked and let's face it, you've had bigger stuff to deal with in recent months," he replied in a matter-of-fact way.

The break-up's been hard but how could I miss this for so long? Cath mused. "That sketch is superb, son... but why have you only sketched half a picture?"

How do I get out of this without giving anything away? "Oh... I ran out of time and didn't want to be late for lunch," Duncan stuttered in reply.

The awkward discussion was broken by noise from the front door. In walked Mary, checking a message on her iPhone and looking her usual, glamorous self. Perfect, polished fake nails with alternating designs adorned her hands and a long blonde ponytail sat perfectly in place, held by a rainbow-coloured scrunchy and a plain headband. A little soft pink lip gloss, small earrings and coordinated casual clothing in pastel colours, completed her 'look'.

As Mary looked in on the kitchen lunch scene, she cattily said, "Oh my, the Undertaker returns. What did you say to Grandad today?"

"None of your business, Nosey Parker, that's private."

"Touched a nerve there then."

Duncan mumbled his excuses, got up and trudged upstairs to the sanctuary of his room. He'd retrieved his graveyard drawing from his mum and tucked his sketch pad securely under his arm.

Once in his room he could hear conversation downstairs about who had unfriended who, plus the up-to-date boyfriend troubles and crushes amongst Mary's peer group.

Duncan had no idea what most of it was about and cared not a jot.

Bigger fish to fry.

He lay back on his bed and held his part-completed sketch up at arm's length and assessed it properly for the first time.

I suppose it is pretty good… but anyway… what happens from here?

After replaying his 'Grandad, CONNECTOR' conversation multiple times in his head, Duncan was no clearer as to what was going to happen but was convinced that he needed to return to the graveyard. It would arouse the suspicions of Cath and Mary if he went back too soon after lunch, so Duncan decided he'd go back after dinner, before it got dark.

Sticking to his plan, Duncan returned to the graveyard with perhaps fifteen to twenty minutes of daylight left. He repeated his rituals of reading the gravestone, saying hi to Grandad Hamish and walking the paths to take his seat on the wooden bench.

Duncan sat quietly but on full alert, intently listening for any voices or movement.

Nothing of note happened for quarter of an hour as the pale evening light turned ever more grey.

Duncan decided that the graveyard was about to get too spooky for comfort. While disappointed not to see or hear anything further, he stood up and headed home for the night.

Did Grandad really speak to me earlier or is this my overactive mind playing tricks on me? There's nothing else for it, I'll come back tomorrow and try again.

After an unsettled night, at 11am on the following morning, Duncan was on his way back to the church yard.

He wiped his nose on a hankie and pulled his waterproof jacket hood up to keep the drizzly rain off his head and face. The weather was grey and depressing so Duncan hoped no one would be around to make him uneasy or overhear anything.

On turning into the graveyard his wishes were granted as he had the place to himself.

Rituals were followed, as always, and a further hankie wipe was required as he read the gold-leaf lettering on his grandparents' gravestone. Duncan was without his sketch pad and pencils today but still made his way over to his usual spot on the wooden bench.

As he sat down, he saw something out of the corner of his eye. There was a distinct capital H, like a hospital sign, carved into the side arm of the wooden bench.

I'm certain that wasn't there yesterday.
I definitely didn't do this.
Is this another sign from Grandad Hamish or just something that's been randomly carved here?

Duncan listened intently, with his eyes peeled, and walked short distances around the bench and gravestone areas for a good half an hour.

There was nothing more.

No voices, no messages, nor other carvings.

He grudgingly said his goodbyes to his grandparents and trudged off home, his damp trainers squeaking as he went.

The rest of the Sunday was routine. Food, some telly, niggling from his mum and sister, a shower after dinner and prep for school, then bed.

Lying on his bed late on, Duncan had another look at his sketch, trying to evoke any new angles on what had happened. As his thoughts eventually drifted towards tomorrow, Monday, the only positive about the ordeal of another school week starting was that he would see Davy.

Should he tell Davy about what had happened, as they shared everything in their loyal gang of two?

No, this was just too big to share for now.

It was vital to hear from Grandad Hamish again before he could consider telling anyone else.

Duncan eventually fell into a fitful sleep, dreaming of voices from beyond the grave and the meaning of a carved capital H.

Chapter 4

The kitchen clock in the McPherson household ticked round to seven-thirty on another grey Monday morning.

"Come on, you pair of lazy bones. School today, so get yourselves moving… sharpish," called Cath.

The lack of noise and movement upstairs indicated her rallying wake-up call had fallen on deaf ears, AGAIN.

"I'm not joking. Get into gear, NOW."

Twenty seconds later a creaking bed spring and a squeaky floorboard provided a hint of movement. The bathroom door clonked shut as Mary took possession of the room, to make herself presentable for her public.

Duncan cosied in and turned over in his bed. *That's me good for at least another fifteen minutes, she takes ages in there.*

Mary didn't quite use up the full fifteen minutes of bathroom time that Duncan had mentally allotted, but she ran it close. Having beautified herself to a satisfactory standard, Mary appeared at her mother's elbow in the kitchen and said, "The Undertaker is still dead to the world up there. What do you reckon the mystery ailment will be today to try and bunk off school?"

"God knows, Mary," Cath replied. "Duncan, get your butt

in gear NOW or I'll ground you."

The younger sibling accepted his fate and awkwardly unfolded his rested limbs out of bed.

In less than a third of the time his sister took, Duncan went through his full morning routine. He was dressed in the Auchterbarn Primary School black and red uniform but looked noticeably uncomfortable in such formal attire. Bits of white shirt tail stuck out, unwittingly, in a couple of places.

He was long-limbed, like his dad, and had dark hair, badly in need of a cut. This was accompanied by a long, narrow face and a toothy grin, when he did in fact smile.

Cath picked up the scent of Lynx deodorant and quietly smiled to herself at her son's standard unkempt look. While a hair out of place to Mary would be the end of the world, the importance placed on appearance by Duncan was close to zero.

"All good this morning, son?" Cath asked as Mary tuned in.

"Yip, I'll get to see Davy and hear how his weekend went."

Mother and daughter both considered this a strangely optimistic Monday morning version of Duncan. He just sat quietly munching his standard bowl of Coco Pops with semi-skimmed milk.

Cath was a receptionist in the local medical practice and worked her hours around the kids' school times. When she checked the wall calendar, she saw a note saying '*Cover an hour for Jean*', scribbled down against today's date.

"Remember, I'm doing an extra hour to cover for Jean today so I'll be a bit later home from work and might not be in when you get back from school. Have you both got your door keys?"

The siblings nodded to indicate that they had their keys, if required.

"What do you fancy for dinner? Pizza?"

Pizza was pretty much the go-to option when Cath was later home from work, so both siblings nodded that pizza was fine by them.

Teeth were then brushed, coats and backpacks picked up. They got kitted up, said cheerio to Mum, went out the front door and down the path to start their school day.

Not far from their door, Mary turned to her younger brother and said in a fake American accent, "See ya later, bro, have a nice day."

She then headed off in the direction of Auchterbarn Secondary School, where she was nearing the end of first year.

Still within Duncan's view, Mary soon met up with some of her group of pals, *The Glam Gang* as Duncan and Davy called them behind their backs.

Duncan loped slowly off then waited on the corner of the next street along. This was where he and Davy met up every school day so they could head in together, strength in numbers against their tormentors.

The terrible twins, Gus and Eric Burgan, were in primary seven and the resident school bullies. They lived on the other side of town, so generally came to school from that direction.

Within a minute or so, Davy shuffled sleepily round the corner, his backpack slung awkwardly over his right shoulder and perked up when he saw his friend waiting for him. Davy was much smaller than Duncan, with wispy blond hair and an almost elf-like appearance. He was painfully quiet and shy, until you got to know him, but was a bright kid with a dry sense of humour. They were an odd-looking pairing but had been firm friends all the way through nursery, then school, and were now in primary six.

The duo said their customary morning hellos and started the walk to school in silence.

Eventually Duncan ventured, "How did your family weekend visit through West go, Davy?"

"It was OK, it's nice to see them but it's pretty boring. We don't go to visit that often although Mum phones and texts them most days," replied Davy.

He went quiet and Duncan thought that was it but then Davy continued, "My folks insist on me going with them to see the olds but they're not very exciting and there's not much to do around where they live. Their house in Kilmarnock is tiny and not in the greatest of areas. They've lived there all their lives and aren't going to move now. The hotel we stayed in and the fancy dinner on Saturday were probably the best bits about the trip. How about you, what did you get up to?"

"Not much really, the weather was pretty nice so I just did some drawing and wandered around a bit, as usual," Duncan replied, hoping the redness appearing on his face and neck, wouldn't betray his lie by omission.

They exchanged further chit-chat while they walked and before long were walking through the school gates. The boys found a quiet corner of the playground to wait for the school bell to indicate the start of the day.

About a minute later, two large, thickset boys with shark-like eyes and glum expressions, lumbered into view at the far side of the playground. An intake of collective breath occurred, as the other pupils felt the oppressive presence of the Burgan boys, Gus and Eric. The well-known bullies for once avoided Davy and Duncan, and moved threateningly towards a small group of primary fours, who were also regular targets of theirs.

"Good weekend, lads? Any wee pressies for us today?" Gus, the older twin by one hour, goaded the cringing younger kids.

Small amounts of cash and sweets were handed over without incident and the bullies moved on, happy with their plunder.

Duncan watched on with anger burning in his chest.

You're going to wonder what's hit you guys once I'm a Connector – this bullying has to stop.

It wasn't long till the school bell rang for the start of classes but in that time Duncan got a fleeting glimpse of his huge crush, Jenny Paterson. His heart leapt in his chest as, in his view, the prettiest girl in the school walked past and joined her 'in crowd' of primary sevens.

Jenny was tallish for her age, had shiny, long, dark hair, with dark brown eyes. She had lovely golden skin, a huge contrast to Duncan's pastiness and was, from her admirer's viewpoint, perfectly proportioned.

God, she's perfect BUT she never gives me so much as a glance.

"Come on, lover boy, let's get in for Registration," said Davy as he tugged at Duncan's elbow, to break his attention away from Jenny Paterson.

Duncan and Davy's class teacher for their primary six year was Ms Robinson (Ms Rowena Angela Robinson to give her full title). Her downbeat, monotone way of checking the attendance register was telling, as it transmitted her lack of enthusiasm towards her charges.

Ms Robinson was in her mid-forties, of medium height and build, and had dark hair set in a bun. She had twenty years of teaching under her belt but appeared quite downtrodden, bored even.

In addition to a very un-sunny disposition, her dowdy and unflattering way of dressing made her look way older than her actual years. Teaching can be tough and rewarding in equal measure but the scales were definitely tipped to *tough*, in Ms Robinson's mind.

The school day continued on its routine way through the morning into lunchtime and on to bell time for going home. Nothing much happened or was learnt.

The day's main points of note from Duncan's perspective were:-
1. No involvement with the Burgan twins.
2. He was fairly sure that Jenny Paterson glanced at him at lunchtime.

Once the school had largely emptied out, Davy and Duncan set forth for home. They wandered slowly out of the school gates and followed their usual route, talking only periodically.

Near their homes, they went their separate ways, and Duncan used his key to let himself in to number twenty-eight. He hung his coat in the hall and contemplated what kind of pizzas Cath would bring home for dinner, as he headed upstairs to his room.

Once in his room, Duncan dropped his backpack on the floor, took his shoes off and pushed them under his bed.

He was instinctively drawn to his sketch pad.

As he flicked the pages open, his heart flipped as there was a drawing. A drawing that *definitely* hadn't been there when he left for school that morning.

The sketched drawing had a strange combination of things

on it:-
- ✓ A tall, tree-covered hill.
- ✓ A dry stone cairn (pile of stones).
- ✓ A full moon in a dark sky.
- ✓ A funny looking, small, hairy creature.

Duncan frantically flicked over to the next page on the pad and there were more – words… no… a poem.

Long before other people knew
I was different, just like you

Not great at chat, or being socially collected
But artistically gifted, and with the Haggi connected

To be a Connector, follow this rule
Go to the Huntsmen Hill cairn, when the moon is set full.

Say your piece, on what gives you trouble,
And Haggi help comes, where the water does bubble

My message is strange, the meaning is deep
So it's very important, our secret to keep!!

Grandad Hamish

Duncan's mind was then a whirlpool of questions. He read, then re-read the poem, over and over. His eyes skimmed between the images of the hill, stone cairn, the moon and the weird creature as he tried to make sense of both the poem and the sketch.

How did Grandad Hamish get this message here?

What's the hairy wee creature, a Haggi?
What does the picture mean?
Is this what you do to be a Connector?

Duncan's concentration was broken by the sound of the front door opening and Mary shouting up to check he was there.

Right, stay calm, keep the sketch and poem away from prying eyes.

"I'm up in my room, Mary, I'll be down in a mo'."

Duncan tore out the two pages with the mysterious drawing and poem on them. He then strained to fold back his mattress and placed the pages on the centre of the base of his bed.

Great care was taken to keep the pages flat, as he knew these were of huge importance.

Chapter 5

Duncan checked the torn out 'message' pages were safely out of view, then wandered downstairs, where Mary was sitting at the kitchen table. She was still in her school uniform and was busy on her iPhone, as usual.

"How did it go today, Dunc?" she asked pleasantly, without looking up or stopping typing on her phone.

"OK, I suppose, nothing much to report," Duncan replied, to avoid getting into a lengthy discussion. "How was your day?"

"Double maths in the morning was a huge drag but I enjoyed music, the practical stuff, getting to play instruments. There weren't any dramas BUT... I think Brad Thomas, the coolest, sexiest guy in our school, might be going to ask me out," replied Mary with a satisfied smirk.

Duncan couldn't believe his youthful ears but decided to play things fairly lightly. "Oh, oh, that's all we need. You, pining over the latest dreamboat. Anyway he's way too old for you, watch yourself there."

"Not a word to Mum," snapped Mary, as Cath opened the front door.

Cath McPherson dumped her handbag on the hall floor

then went back out of the half-open front door, to her Nissan Qashqai on the drive. She lifted something from her car then re-entered with hunger-inducing smells coming from three pizza boxes.

"Wow, smells fab. What toppings did you get, Mum?" asked Mary enthusiastically.

"Meat feast and American hot for us to share and plain old margarita for your fusspot brother."

Plates, cutlery and condiments were quickly assembled on the kitchen table and the feast began, without any ceremony.

Cath provided her news update as they ate.

One of the current doctors at her practice was moving away, so they were advertising for a new doctor to replace her. Jean, one of the other receptionists, had had a tough couple of days and had to put her cat down at the vet. Cath tried to lighten the mood and asked, "So how did you guys get on at school today?"

Duncan replied exactly as he had to his sister earlier.

Mary did likewise but omitted the bit about the potential new boyfriend, as she glared at her brother, daring him to say anything.

They all munched away in relative silence, enjoying their pizza.

As Duncan finished up his last slice, he was itching to get out to go to the graveyard to see if he could contact Grandad Hamish for more details.

His heart sank as he heard the wind picking up and rattling the window. There was a distinct stormy feel in the air so Duncan stared out into the distance, looking west/south-west, where the wind and weather were coming from. The huge mass of swirling grey and black cloud that he saw, looked like it was bringing the end of the world straight to Auchterbarn. It certainly didn't look like a passing shower and would not be going off any time soon.

While it wasn't what he wanted to do, the common-sense approach was to postpone visiting the graveyard until after school tomorrow.

So that's what he did.

After helping with the dishes and tidying up, Duncan told Cath he was going upstairs to do his homework and bumped, frustratedly, up the stairs to his room.

Half an hour later, the rain was still battering off the windows. It was so dark and wild outside, it looked like the middle of a winter's night.

Duncan was oblivious, deep in thought.

If Grandad can get messages onto the sketch pad then maybe if I write questions on it, he'll reply!

Convincing himself that his idea could work, Duncan set about coming up with suitable questions.

After long deliberation, he opened his sketch pad nearer the unused back pages.

He wrote:-

Hi Grandad, thanks for your message.
I think I follow most of how to make CONTACT but exactly when, where and how do I do it?
Do I speak direct to a Haggi?
Also not sure what to say – any suggestions?

After completing his message, so as not to seem too anti-social, Duncan went downstairs and watched some television with his mum and sister.

After a better sleep than of late, the next day's school routine started the same as always.

Duncan was distracted throughout the whole school day. His mind was firmly on a reply on his sketch pad and not Ms Robinson's monotonous teachings.

After a tortuously slow afternoon, Duncan finally said goodbye to Davy at the street corner and hurried back to number twenty-eight.

Cath's car was already in the drive when Duncan got to the house. They exchanged small updates from their respective days and Duncan then headed up to his room. The anticipation for a reply was overwhelming but he was also hesitant about checking, in case there was no reply.

Duncan's prayers were answered as there, on the page under his questions, was a short message.

Wait till after lights out, then open the medal of honour, which is inside your pillowcase.
Ask it your questions. You'll then be clear on what is required.
Just be yourself. Good luck.
Grandad Hamish

Duncan felt a surge of adrenaline but didn't want to go against the instructions. He wouldn't take the box out of his pillowcase immediately, but needed to know if it actually existed.

He ran his hand round the pillowcase to make sure it was in place.

It was there. *Yeessss. Just need to wait till bedtime, then it's action stations.*

Time seemed to stop for Duncan but eventually his mum popped her head round the door to say goodnight and let him know Mary was already away to bed. He held his impatience in check for another hour then decided the girls would be asleep.

His hand touched the felt-covered box in the pillowcase and lifted it free. Duncan's first idea was to open the box under the bed covers so the sound would be muted when speaking. This thought was blown out of the water, as the bright light that flooded out almost blinded Duncan in the confined space.

He closed the lid and took the box over towards his window and away from the door nearest the corridor. This time round, Duncan opened the box gradually and allowed his eyes time to adjust to the spectacular multi-coloured light. He marvelled at its beauty and hypnotic power for several minutes before remembering that he could ask questions.

In a very muffled voice Duncan held a short, surreal discussion with the strange voice from the medal of honour/light box.

His questions were answered and his mission was made clear.
- ✓ He was to go alone to the cairn on Huntsmen Hill under darkness.
- ✓ A successful Connection can only be made on one of the two nights leading up to a full moon (and preferably on a clear night).
- ✓ The next full moon is due next Thursday (so he had over a week to prepare).
- ✓ Once at the cairn, stand one pace due north and clearly state, in your own words, why you're there.
- ✓ A Haggi will be listening and your Connection assessed.

Yet again, young Duncan's mind was whirling all ways and a sleepless night was very likely.

Chapter 6

Duncan actually slept better than he had expected, although he'd only got about four hours' kip before he heard Cath shouting his wake-up call. He vividly remembered the magic light and Connection instructions of the night before but decided to play sleepy at breakfast.

He would start his plan later.

After breakfast, the siblings gathered their backpacks, said goodbye to their mother and headed off to school.

Davy always paid attention to his pal but he thought Duncan seemed even more detached than usual on a very quiet walk to another day of learning. Duncan was oblivious to his perceived detachment, as his brain mulled over a plan for his Connector trip up Huntsmen Hill. He still had over a week to prepare but needed to use the time wisely so that 'Operation Full Moon' (as he'd named it) ran smoothly.

Duncan switched off from Ms Robinson's ramblings and used the time on more pressing matters.

He made up a mental checklist, in no particular order, of all the things he'd need to consider.

1. Torch.
2. Getting out of the house and back in (without being

rumbled) – open window, ladder?
3. Substitute Dunc body?
4. What to wear?
5. How long will it take, up and back?
6. Notebook and pen
7. Get Davy to help?
8. Binoculars? – No use at night.

Duncan was convinced that item 5 was key to the planning but the biggest challenges were items 2 and 3 on his list.

He needed to get out, and back in, without discovery.

Duncan had briefly considered a sleepwalking episode as an excuse for being out in the middle of the night but rejected this as unlikely to be believable.

It was also necessary to make it look like he was asleep in his bed, when he wasn't.

His mum's routine on a school night rarely varied. When Cath locked up downstairs and headed up to bed, she almost always popped her head round the kids' doors to check they were in bed/asleep. She also had a habit of getting up around four in the morning for a night-time pee, courtesy of childhood bladder issues. When this happened, she would repeat her earlier check by looking into their rooms.

On the way home from school, Duncan decided that walking the Huntsmen Hill route in daylight would assist in the planning. The forecast for tonight was horrible so he committed to do this tomorrow night after dinner, while it was still light.

Duncan had discarded the idea of asking Davy to help in Operation Full Moon. He didn't want to block out his best pal completely though, so he asked him to go with him on his evening walking recce. Davy agreed to go with Duncan the following night but without an inkling of the real reason behind their route.

On the Thursday night, the two friends enjoyed their walk up and down Huntsmen Hill with Duncan chatting more freely than he had in the last couple of days. Despite appearances, he was also checking the time taken and the details of the route, VERY closely.

Once they were back at their meeting point corner, the boys said their farewells and headed for their respective homes.

Duncan exchanged small talk with his mum and sister, watched TV for a few minutes then, sewing the behavioural seeds for Operation Full Moon, said he was tired and heading for bed.

After assessing the travel time and adding in some contingency, Duncan had a more complete basis for Operation Full Moon.

He had decided that he'd like to avoid the wee small hours. His preferred option was to leave his house around bedtime, if not before; get up there, do what needed done. The key aim was to be back in bed long before Cath's likely check during her standard four a.m. toilet visit.

He still needed to work out the how but nothing of note came into his head and he drifted off to sleep.

The following day, Friday, at morning break, a pupil randomly mentioned a teacher 'wearing a syrup'. Duncan initially wasn't listening properly but tuned in to the follow-up discussion. This revealed that a 'syrup' was rhyming slang for a wig (i.e. syrup of figs = wigs, therefore syrup = wig).

A lightbulb went on in Duncan's head as the seed of an idea popped into his brain.

Use your artistic abilities, it's time to get creative.

From somewhere deep in his brain, Duncan remembered Grandad Hamish telling him a story about a daring and famous prison escape. A group of prisoners had, incredibly, managed to escape from the infamous Alcatraz prison.

The prison is on an island near the Golden Gate Bridge and about a mile offshore from San Francisco, USA. The escapee prisoners in Alcatraz had a very similar issue to Duncan for Operation Full Moon. They had to appear to be in their cells, asleep in their beds, when the prison guards did their night-time rounds in semi-darkness. To achieve this they created model human heads out of papier-mâché. They then added paint to the model to define dark hair and some basic human features.

On the night of their escape, the prisoners had placed cushions and clothes under the bed covers, to make them look like a sleeping body. The painted papier-mâché heads were then placed on the respective pillows, to look like real heads.

The ruse worked perfectly and the missing prisoners weren't noticed until the following morning. Their solution was ingenious and Duncan decided he was going to copy them, with one additional flourish. He would use a wig, as his hair had too much volume to be credible in only paint.

During the Friday lunch break, Duncan left school and went to a charity shop. He quickly found what he was looking for and paid a small fee for a wig, which almost exactly matched his hair colour.

Duncan put the wig in his backpack and headed back to school. He got there with plenty time to spare but was apprehended by the dreaded Burgan twins.

"Where have you been, Skinny Malinky?" taunted Gus.

"Just at a shop," Duncan replied.

"Well then, you must have cash to burn, so hand it over or you'll get battered," said Gus.

"I think a pound each, would be acceptable to avoid a pasting," added Eric.

Duncan burned inside with hatred of these two. He was also ashamed of his own cowardice but was genuinely scared of trying to resist their demands.

He reluctantly handed over two pound coins with a limp hand.

"Nice doing business with you," said the twins in unison, as they turned and lumbered off in search of their next target.

Duncan felt dreadful after meekly handing over his cash and couldn't face meeting up with Davy. He walked dejectedly into the school building with his head bowed and went to one of his sanctuaries, the girls' toilet.

No one will bother me in here.

Duncan sat in a toilet cubicle with his feet pulled up onto the toilet seat. No visible feet reduced the chances of detection in his mind. There were no confrontations or awkward scenes at a boy being in the girls' loo, and the bell rang for afternoon classes to begin.

The only highlight of the afternoon, for Duncan, was a massive positive coincidence.

Just before home time, Ms Robinson announced with very little enthusiasm, that over the next two days in class, they would be doing an art project. *Making papier-mâché figures.*

Duncan's heart felt immediately lighter as his luck changed and part of the plan for Operation Full Moon landed right in his lap.

Davy looked less than enthused and slumped wearily at the news. *I'm just rubbish at art, not like Dunc, he's awesome.*

On the walk home their respective moods didn't alter and there wasn't much chat. They went their separate ways at the usual place and Duncan headed round to number twenty-eight.

The house was empty as he let himself in.

That's odd – Mum didn't say anything this morning, about working late.

His confusion was soon cleared up, as there was a note from Cath on the kitchen unit.

Picking Mary up from school and taking her out for a milkshake and a girlie chat.
I'll sort dinner once we're home.
Mum Xx

Aha – time to consider my escape plan with no one around.

He was now pretty sure that his body and papier-mâché head deception would be ready before Thursday night. However, he still needed to test and decide on a suitable entry and exit plan.

Duncan had considered using a ladder against the wall, where his bedroom window was, for getting out and back in again.

There were flaws with this idea, though.

1. They didn't already have a ladder that was big enough.
2. Even if he had the funds, how could he explain the purchase?
3. There was a high(ish) risk of noise.
4. If he got back in, he'd still have to go out again (either during the night or early the next morning) to move it and avoid giving the game away.

IDEA REJECTED.

He made his way up the stairs to his room to dump his backpack and change into more comfortable clothes. On the fifth step, the floorboard loudly creaked.

These stairs were going to be a major stumbling block in his plan.

Chapter 7

Later that Friday evening, the girlie chat that Cath had referred to in her kitchen note had taken place. It had been the standard 'concerned worldly-wise mother' versus 'about to be teenage daughter' chat. Warnings of the big bad world and all that could go wrong, were delivered from the mum side. Rolling of the eyes and the "I'm not a baby. What's your problem? I know what I'm doing," stance from the youngster.

The milkshakes were drunk but the chat didn't go as well as Cath had hoped.

The car journey home was undertaken in a stony silence, only broken by an offer and subsequent refusal of fish and chips.

Duncan was in his room when the front door opened and his mum called him down for dinner.

"Fish supper from the chippy, Dunc, come and get it."

When he got downstairs, Mary had a face like thunder, so Duncan didn't bother trying to speak to her. He was also savvy enough to know not to ask Cath about the girlie chat over milkshakes.

Cath said, "Tuck in. Oh, remember your dad's coming

tomorrow morning to take you both out."

With all that had been going on, Duncan had completely forgotten that his dad was supposed to be coming tomorrow. It would be one of his irregular visits, if he could drag himself away from work and/or 'The Bitch'.

Duncan's first instinct was that he could well do without the visit, as he didn't get much out of meeting his dad. In addition, it would impact on precious planning time for Operation Full Moon.

Friday night in the McPherson household passed off, without anything of note happening. The sun went down, the moon came out, the sun came up again and Saturday morning duly arrived.

It was a grey but dry day with a moderate breeze.

Mary and Dunc were both up and ready in plenty of time, ahead of their dad's agreed pick-up time of eleven a.m.

At nine-twenty, Cath's mobile rang and George dropped the bombshell that he was cancelling (AGAIN). As soon as Mary picked up on the cancellation, she burst into tears and curled up on the living room sofa.

So as to be able to immediately console her daughter, Cath cut the call after saying she'd call George back. She sat down beside her daughter and held her tight.

Duncan suddenly felt like an intruder, so awkwardly exited and sat on the landing stairs so he was not in the room but could still listen in. In amongst the tears and frustration, Duncan could, just about, make out Mary sobbing and saying, "He doesn't love me anymore. We're nothing to him."

Duncan was not prone to shows of emotion but, in that moment, he did feel truly sorry for his big sister. He also realised that she wasn't as self-assured and confident as he thought she was. *She's actually human and has issues like we all do.*

Duncan started to get up from his listening post on the stairs. As he did so, he pressed his hands down at each side of him to provide some leverage.

The fifth floorboard didn't creak like it had previously.

Another lightbulb popped on in Duncan's brain as the final part of Operation Full Moon fell into place.

I'm good to go.

A quarter of an hour had passed since the cancellation call from George. Cath had calmed Mary down a lot but she remained puffy eyed and teary, as she'd taken herself off to her room.

Cath went into the kitchen and called George back on his mobile. Deep-rooted anger coursed through her as she demanded, "So, what's your excuse this time, George?"

"It's not an excuse. I have to meet a new client for a big contract and it needs me to handle it as the boss," offered George.

"Clients and contracts trump your kids every time," added Cath, cuttingly.

"But I pay you plenty for them," responded a defensive George.

Cath went off on frustrated rant. "It's not about money, it's about time… quality, invested time… in YOUR kids. Mary's crying her heart out in her room and thinks you don't love her anymore with your constant call-offs and rejections. And Duncan… He might seem unconcerned to you… but he's way sharper than he gets credit for. He notices lots of things but just doesn't say anything. Dunc does what he does and retreats into his protective shell. Tell you what, George, just forget your own flesh and blood. Go to hell… Just go and meet your very important client, it's obvious where your priorities lie."

The big-shot architect needed no further encouragement and speedily ended the call.

Chapter 8

Duncan had kept a low profile on the back of George's weekend visit cancellation and the following few days at school. He needed to avoid distractions and conserve energy for the big day.

There had been a lot of tiptoeing on eggshells around his sister, plus dodging the dreaded Burgan bullies. The creative side in him had, however, enjoyed two days of glorious art work in class, which motivated him like never before. He'd even got glowing comments for his papier-mâché work from Ms Robinson.

Duncan opened his sleepy eyes at the sound of Cath's regular morning wake-up call. He took a few seconds to 'shake awake', and started to buzz from the realisation that Thursday, the day of Operational Full Moon, had finally arrived.

Duncan wished he had a time machine and could just zoom forward to night-time. Regrettably, he had to spend the day at school.

The normal daily routine had been followed, he and Davy had avoided the bullies, thus far, and they were at their respective desks in class. The hands on Ms Robinson's classroom clock appeared to be fixed in concrete, with every second seeming to last for a week.

Despite a welcome glance of the lovely Jenny Paterson at lunchtime (she didn't see him, as usual), the uneventful day dragged, badly. After a very long afternoon of clock watching, the home bell finally rang and the relieved pupils started to exit. Duncan had taken his completed dummy papier-mâché head home the day before. It was safely hidden in his room and ready to be used, wig and all.

Once they were all home in number twenty-eight, the McPherson family unit chatted a bit, ate dinner and did usual stuff.

However, this was no 'usual' night.

Duncan was bursting to get started on Operation Full Moon so, earlier than his normal bed time, he feigned tiredness, said goodnight and headed up to his room. He cleverly bumped the living room door closed a little so it would obstruct lines of sight elsewhere in the house. Duncan then deliberately clomped up the stairs so it was obvious to Mary, and especially Cath, that he'd gone up. He then made a noisy demonstration that he'd been into the toilet and brushed his teeth.

As the night explorer went into his bedroom, he switched the light on, then drew the curtains back. A big, bright, beautiful Full Moon shone down, in all its splendour.

Operation Full Moon was ON.

Duncan had managed to gather some extra pillows and cushions on the sly and he set them out, under his bed covers, to simulate his body. The dummy head was then retrieved from its hiding place and placed in exactly the right spot to align with the 'body'.

Duncan tiptoed over to the light switch and put it off. He

then looked across at his body double in the bed and reviewed it with a critical eye to see if it would work.

After some consideration, he moved the dummy's head a fraction, then rechecked it. He decided it was as good as it was going to be and would stand scrutiny, from a distance. So long as Cath didn't actually come into the room, it should be fine.

He then put on his chosen dark-coloured clothing and trainers to go into his 'ninja' mode. He took a small note pad and a pencil from the drawer, in case he needed to write anything down during the Connection. A torch was already in his pocket.

Once satisfied that he had everything he needed, Duncan quietly made his way to his bedroom door then out into the corridor.

He stood very still and intently listened.

Faint female voices could be heard from the living room.

The TV programme sound overlaid this but he was fairly certain that both Mary and his mum were there, downstairs.

Stretching his legs very wide, as if doing a yoga stretch, Duncan moved stealthily, both feet right into the sides of the corridor. He successfully negotiated this and had progressed, noiselessly, to the second from bottom stair, when he heard Mary saying goodnight to Cath.

Oh no – hurry, man, or you're caught.

Duncan moved as quickly and quietly as he could onto the ground floor then dashed round the back of the downstairs office door, and stood absolutely still. He hadn't bumped anything and his breathing wasn't too loud, so he hoped he'd got away with it.

Seconds later Mary opened the living room door and headed upstairs to bed, with a stifled yawn.

One down, one to go.

Duncan didn't want to risk going out the front door until Cath had gone to bed, as the door often caught and made a racket, plus the way out was visible from Cath's seat in the living room.

He waited fifteen anxious minutes then heard movement. Duncan listened intently, senses on full alert.

The TV is still on, it's a pee break, not bedtime. Time to GO.

As Cath disappeared into the downstairs loo, she instinctively closed the door behind her. As soon as the loo door closed, Duncan stealthily opened the front door, checked he had his key for getting back in, and exited without much noise.

He then hustled down the path and off along the street.

By the time Cath called it a night, it was after eleven o'clock. She followed her usual routine and after visiting the toilet, popped her head round Duncan's bedroom door to check on him. Cath didn't hear any snoring but saw a dark-haired figure lying very still in the bed, presumably sleeping. She quietly said, "Sleep well, Dunc," then turned to head for Mary's room, unaware that she'd just wished pleasant dreams to a papier-mâché dummy.

As Cath headed for Mary's room to wish her goodnight, her son was already close to Huntsmen Hill.

Duncan was bubbling with nervous energy as he skipped over a stile onto the historic shepherds' trail. Although he'd done a trial run and was confident of where he was going, that was in daylight, not under time pressure, and with a normal heart rate. He continued to make his way carefully, upwards, using the moonlight and stars to check his position, the way ahead and to avoid any trips.

There was a small, but powerful torch in his pocket although he didn't want to use it, unless he had to, as someone might see the light and be suspicious.

Duncan arrived at a dark spot surrounded by trees, blocking out the moonlight. He stopped to take a breather and as he did so, an owl made a hooting noise. The intrepid explorer nearly jumped out of his skin.

Just as he was getting his breath back, he tripped over something spiky and lost his balance.

What the heck was that?

A stray hedgehog, shuffled into the loose foliage. Totally spooked, Duncan righted himself from his hedgehog trip.

He had taken less than fifty further, very cautious steps when a sudden disturbance in the bushes made Duncan spin round in panic. A loud shuffling sound poured out from the undergrowth to his right.

His heart was beating like a sledgehammer and his brain buzzing with all sorts of wild thoughts.

Calm down, Dunc, it's not the road to Oz, there's no lions and tigers and bears in Scotland.

He stood, static, and it became still and eerily quiet. Duncan eventually moved on and the trees thinned out.

Once the moonlight reappeared, Duncan looked back and saw the bright white on the face of a badger, which was watching him quizzically.

That's a relief – MOVE!

He pressed on up the steepening path and paused for breath again, near a crest on the upward slope. As the young McPherson gazed upwards, he could make out many stars and recognised the cluster of seven in the Plough/Big Dipper constellation.

With breathing regulated, he started moving again.

It was only another two minutes till he breached the crest and there in front of him was his destination.

The moonlit, stone cairn on Huntsmen Hill.

Duncan was a little overwhelmed and flustered, unsure of his next steps. He mentally went through a list of the various instructions he'd got from Grandad Hamish, his sketch book and the mysterious, beautiful Medal of Honour.

Confident that he now knew what to do, Duncan made his way right up to the brightly lit cairn. The stone was really beautiful close up but Duncan was not to be distracted, now he'd got this far. He looked down at his watch and checked due north.

Dunc shuffled about ninety degrees around the cairn, then stopped and checked the compass bearing again.

Spot on.

The latest Connector took one pace back and knew he was in place to say his piece. The following awkward and unrehearsed speech came out of Duncan's mouth.

"I'm not much good with words but I'll do my best. My name is Duncan McPherson. My Grandad Hamish knows that I'm different to a lot of other kids and that I have a tough time at school. He's been guiding me and led me here through messages and drawings, so that I can connect and obtain your help. I'm not brave, tough or daring but I've had enough of doing nothing. It's time for me to take a stand against bad stuff and I'd really be grateful for your help. Thank you."

After he stopped speaking, a heavy block of cloud blew across the moon, on the moderate, prevailing WSW wind and the previously bright moonlight disappeared. A sudden eerie darkness took over and Duncan felt very alone, high on the hill, when he should be tucked up safely in bed.

He wasn't sure what he should do now.

Wait around? Shout out? Or just leave?

Hamish hadn't given him any details beyond how to relay his message.

Based on the lack of any noise or movement, plus his growing apprehension, Duncan made up his mind to go home and wait for further contact. The moon remained hidden so he switched on his torch, to be able to check where he was walking. Duncan then cautiously started back to the trail to go back down Huntsmen Hill.

He was wholly unaware that a busy pair of eyes and ears had been watching and listening, from high up in a nearby tree.

His message had, very definitely, been heard.

Duncan made it safely back home about fifty-five minutes before his mum's usual nocturnal toilet visit. He used his key to let himself in, making sure he moved as slowly and quietly as possible. The stairs were safely negotiated, with his feet wide spread, as had worked before. He made no creaks on the floorboards, was soon along the corridor and into his room.

YEEESSS, I've done it.

Duncan undressed and two minutes later had taken the place of his body double in his bed.

He might be in bed but there was little chance of sleep till the huge buzz of the night's events left his body.

Forty-seven minutes later, Duncan was still wide awake when he heard movement. Soon after, he quickly shut his eyes in fake sleep, as his bedroom door creaked open and his mum's head appeared round the door to check on him.

Chapter 9

Mary was sat at the kitchen table, ready for school. School wasn't what was on her mind though. She read, then re-read a message on her iPhone. Then she read it another couple of times to confirm the words in the text, which she'd received through the night.

Mary had a warm, tingly buzz in her belly and a grin like the Cheshire Cat from Wonderland. Her fingers moved at lightning speed, and her false nails clicked on the screen, as she typed messages to the Glam Gang.

Cath was too busy bustling around to notice, as she scrambled, irritably, to get everyone ready and out, to start their Friday activities.

Mary almost dropped her phone in fright as Cath roared, "Dunc, get your butt down here sharpish."

Duncan was experiencing the energy dip that follows a massive high. This was not helped by his very limited sleep time last night.

He'd tentatively opened his eyes when he registered Cath's 'get up for school' shout. A few seconds later, the memories of Operation Full Moon came flashing back into his mind. With a casual smirk to himself, he dragged himself out of bed.

He did his bathroom stint and arrived in the kitchen, in uniform, within seven minutes of Cath's roared request.

As Duncan sat down to eat his Coco Pops, Cath registered how bleary eyed her son looked.

"My god, you look rough, son. That's what an all-night session does for you," she offered, her mood lightening slightly.

Play it cool, Dunc, she doesn't have a clue about last night.

"Nah, I just didn't sleep much and feel like I might be coming down with some bug."

Cath put her hand flat on his forehead. "Doesn't feel like you're burning up or anything, you're going to school… I'm not falling for that old trick. Anyway, when I checked on you at bed time, you were sparked out like a fallen log."

Duncan just ignored her and slurped up the last of the milk and cereal from the bowl. As he finished up, Duncan glanced at Mary and was surprised to see her looking so bright on a school morning.

The school pupils got their stuff together, said goodbye to Cath and went out the front door and down the path together. Once out of earshot, Mary pulled Duncan round by the shoulder, so he was facing her. She looked like she was going to pop with happiness and said to Duncan, with machine gun delivery, "Brad Thomas has only gone and… asked ME… out. I'm meeting him next Friday at half-seven. The girls are gonna be sooo envious. It's going to be the best night of my life. You've not said anything to Mum about Brad, have you?"

"No, it's none of my business but I don't think going on a date with him is a good idea," Duncan responded, bluntly.

"You're just sooo square. See you later, bro."

Duncan shook his head wearily at his sister's revelation, as she skipped away to meet the Glam Gang. He wandered round the corner to meet Davy and was surprised to see his pal was already waiting for him. Duncan distractedly told him about Mary's latest revelation from the world of boys. Davy smiled, shrugged, then went quiet for a bit.

He eventually said, "Weather's supposed to be good tomorrow. Fancy a good old wander around, just us?"

"Yeh, sounds good, just meet at the corner, about ten?"

"Perfect."

There wasn't much more chat on their journey and the odd-looking duo made it to school on time. There was no sighting of Jenny Paterson, which was disappointing to Duncan, but there was also the upside that the Burgan twins didn't show face by the time the bell rang.

Within twenty minutes of lessons starting, Duncan was disengaged from proceedings. Ms Robinson was doing a history session and actually trying to engage, which was unusual. Duncan was elsewhere, his brain muddling over what his next steps should be, to follow up on last night.

Did the Haggi get my message?

Is this whole thing a giant wind-up?

Will they come to me?

Do I need to leave another message on the sketch pad?

Ms Robinson, for once, noticed that Duncan was not participating, as he stared out the window.

"And what are your thoughts on my last point, young Duncan?"

"Sorry, Miss, I was miles away." He stated the obvious in reply.

Ms Robinson had made her point and resumed her ramblings. As she did so Davy was looking over at Duncan, rather than seeking history knowledge. Duncan returned to his mind mapping and then thought of something.

There was something in the poem, what was it about help?

The sketch and poem were very familiar to Duncan but he'd sort of moved on from these as he focused on Operation Full Moon. He tried to recall the words over and over, till eventually it clicked.

Say your piece on what gives you trouble,
And Haggi help comes, where the water does bubble.

There's lots of water around here but could this mean the local burn?

The bell for morning break broke Duncan out of his mind games.

Davy smiled over at him and they headed out into the playground for some fresh air.

The Burgan bullies came by and rattled their cage a bit but the quiet friends had no money or goodies to offer so, remarkably, the twins let it slide without violence, saying, "Double next time."

During the lunch break, over at Auchterbarn Secondary School, Mary held centre stage with the other three members of the Glam Gang. All the girls were all in the same school year although none had a birthday in the same month. Two of them, Steph and Ash, were in a different class to the others. They had got Mary's numerous, love-struck texts earlier but had also spoken to Mary as they walked to school. However, Mary had been gushing, almost hyperventilating, as she rabbited on about how the wonderfully gorgeous Brad had asked her out. Therefore, they didn't know much more than the info in the texts.

Di had got Mary's texts too but lived on the other side of town. She was in Mary's class but hadn't had time to chat to her due to being late that morning.

The four members of the Glam Gang were now in the library, which wasn't busy, on the pretence that they were researching a school project. Technically, this wasn't a lie. The project was Brad Thomas and Mary was the very willing pupil.

"From your messages, we know he asked you out, last night, BY TEXT. Has he contacted you since?" asked Di (Diane) Davidson. Di was the tallest of the Glam Gang, with a long, pale face, matching her overall body shape and colouring. She had green eyes and medium-length, strawberry-blonde hair. Not a classic beauty but pretty in her own way. Di was by far the most streetwise and shrewdest of the Gang, probably due to having three older brothers.

"Well… no… but that doesn't matter, I'm sure he's been busy," replied Mary.

According to my big brother he's been very busy indeed, thought Di, but didn't say anything to burst her friend's bubble.

"Where are you meeting him?" asked Ash (Ashleigh) Sinclair.

*

Ash was a bubbly girl, well developed for her age, with lovely blue eyes and rosy cheeks, providing colour against her light-hued hair. She was loyal and dependable, an only child, and was the one member of the Glam Gang with a current boyfriend.

"In Grange Park at half-seven. I don't know what we're doing but I know what I'd like to do," Mary replied to Ash, playing things up a bit to make her sound more mature than she was.

"I heard Brad's mum's a right alki, always steaming drunk, and his dad was a womaniser, long gone now. He might not have much of a home life," ventured Steph (Stephanie) Findlay, a blonde girl with model-like looks and a famous ex-footballer dad, who lashed cash on his only child's every whim. Steph had been Mary's bestie since nursery school. She was a very girly girl and fairly bright, although not very worldly wise.

Mary replied to Steph's question with full gusto and bravado. "I'm not bothered about his home life, I just want HIM. Anyway my dad doesn't care a jot about us. He's away spending his cash on his bimbo. My mum's always on my case about not doing anything I'll regret. And… I've got a weird brother… so my home life is no great selling point, either."

"Aye but your mum loves you and looks out for you," retorted Steph.

"Yea right, she's just jealous that she got dumped and can't attract a man but I CAN."

"Meow – Little Miss Cat Claws. That's unfair, your mum's sound."

"You don't have to live with her. Anyway, Di, you're the sensible one, what do you reckon?"

"If I'm honest, M, he's bad news and too old for you. He's sixteen and you're not quite thirteen. That's a huge deal at our age."

"I took Brad's picture this morning, when he wasn't looking, he's just so sexy," said Mary, swooning over the photo, displaying up from her phone. She then continued. "He's not like some old paedo with a dirty old man raincoat… or an online groomer… he's a PUPIL at our school," spluttered Mary in defence of her new man. "And you, Ash, what's your take?"

"I'm not sure you want my view as it isn't very positive. This guy just sounds too much of a wild card."

"Christ almighty, you're all loved up with Brian, Mr Reliable. Your life's not exactly rock and roll."

"I'm perfectly happy with Brian, I'm not necessarily expecting marriage, kids and happy ever after but at least he's solid and only a year older, not a cradle snatcher."

Mary had had enough. She jumped up in a strop, said, "Sod the lot of you," then marched out of the library, petulantly banging the door as she stormed out.

"That went well," commented Di.

The three girls shrugged, got up and quietly left the library.

As the bell rang to indicate the start of the afternoon session, Mary was already in her classroom seat, with tears of hurt and frustration welling up in her eyes. She felt deflated and disappointed with her friends' responses to her wonderful news. She thought they'd have been more supportive of her.

Well screw them. I'll be with Brad and show them.

The other three members of the Glam Gang had decided that things needed smoothing over. They all texted Mary, apologised and offered an olive branch suggestion of a quick milkshake get-together on the way home. Mary was still raw from the library exchange but agreed to a Glam Gang get-together after school.

Steph and Ash were waiting just outside the main school door, as Di and a still-angry Mary came out into the milky afternoon light.

Lunchtime events were still casting a cloud so there wasn't much chat on the way to Christina's, one of the local cafés. After ordering, they sat down round a table for four.

Di opened the peace talks with a heartfelt and mature speech. "M, you are perfectly entitled to make your own choices in life. You asked our views on things and we replied honestly, as good pals do. It's obvious you disagree with our take on things but we're just looking out for you. We've got too many years invested in each other to fall out about anything, no matter what that is. How about, the three of us button it for the time being and you have your date with Brad. Then you tell us ALL about it? Pals truce?"

Mary's face brightened and she ushered the girls to her, with beckoning hand movements. They stood up and folded into a four-way group hug.

The Glam Gang was restored, at least for now.

Duncan was already home from school and loitering on the stairs, as Mary came in. With one quick glance, he could tell her buoyant mood of this morning was long gone.

Cath also sensed hostility so tried to defuse things by saying, "It's not a big deal but why didn't you let me know you'd be a bit later home from school?"

"I got distracted and forgot, alright," snapped Mary.

"OK, we were worried about you but you're here safe now and that's what matters."

The discussion was left at that and Mary went to her bedroom for some 'quiet time'.

Cath made dinner for all three of them and she ate her meal with Duncan. She chatted a bit about her work and asked how school had been but she could tell Duncan's mind was elsewhere.

He tidied up and did the dishes, then went out for a short walk to get some air. Duncan had decided earlier to try the den area at the burn in case of any Haggi contact.

His trip to the den went without sight or sound of any mystery creatures, so Duncan turned along the bank of the burn and wandered home. By the time he came back in, Mary had emerged from her 'quiet time' and was just finishing a plate of the sweet chilli chicken stir fry that Cath had made earlier.

As she put her knife and fork down, Mary said, "Thanks, Mum, that was really nice. I'm sorry for being snappy earlier."

The younger sibling thought it would be prudent to keep out of the way, so he left the girls to it and went to his room.

The newfound calm downstairs didn't last long. Within five minutes there were raised voices and some unpleasant things were said. Duncan heard an almighty bang as his sister slammed her room door shut, after storming up the stairs.

In the lyrics of the Nat King Cole song, THERE MAY BE TROUBLE AHEAD.

Chapter 10

On the Saturday, as agreed the day before, the double D duo had spent several hours together, in the great outdoors. Duncan was just relieved to be out of the house and not having to deal with the fallout from last night's verbal scrap between his mum and older sister.

Grandad Hamish's trusty old binoculars hung round Duncan's neck so they could better watch and check for wildlife. As they had walked, crocus, daffodils and a few early bluebells were visible here and there as the plant life emerged from winter.

While wandering aimlessly around the countryside, they'd spotted several robins and a hovering kestrel, waiting to pounce on an unsuspecting victim. They'd also seen two foxes, several deer and a lot of dogs, mostly accompanied by their walkers.

They'd done their bit for the environment, picking up discarded plastic bottles and cans, which they put into recycling bins on their way home in the late afternoon.

There hadn't been much in the way of chat, just two outsiders happy to be free of hassles and in their own quiet company. Despite their comfortable togetherness, Duncan had wrestled with telling Davy about the whole Haggi saga of the last few days. Although his friend was completely oblivious, Davy was also harbouring hard things to discuss. He stayed quiet, however, as he always did.

Come the Sunday morning, Duncan had a long lie-in to make up for his sporadic night-time sleep. Once he was eventually up, fed and dressed, he'd headed out without calling on Davy, simply feeling the need to be by himself.

He'd just about come to terms with the need to keep his only pal in the dark about the various strange events of recent times.

But why do I still feel bad about it?

It was an unusually warm Sunday for Scotland at this time of year, as Duncan arrived at one of his favourite outdoor 'lazing' places in a wee secluded sun trap. It was in a horseshoe shape, closed in and protected by very jaggy gorse bushes but with the short, open end providing a bird's-eye view of the burn. The only clear access was via a narrow strip of grass, along the bank of the burn.

The morning dew had long since dried up and the grass was quite lush and comfy. Knowing this was a safe spot, Duncan dropped his fishing rod then settled down to rest and check out the water and watch out for wildlife.

It must have been really comfy as, within five minutes, Duncan fell sound asleep. He eventually woke with a start, woken by his own snoring.

He was a bit disorientated, at first, but after a few seconds his senses suddenly sparked into overdrive.

There's definitely something or somebody watching me.

He scanned around and eventually noticed a shadow, the size of maybe a child or a decent-sized dog, coming from behind a gorse bush, near the edge of the burn.

A strong but non-threatening voice then spoke.

"Dinnae be fiert, Duncan, ma name's Hannibal, 'n' Ah'm a Haggi warrior, pronounced HAG – EYE. Ah'm here tae help, eftir yer moonlight cairn visit."

To Duncan's utter astonishment, a wee furry creature, partially clad in tartan clothes, stepped into his horseshoe 'den'. As Hannibal took a couple of steps nearer, the Haggi politely removed his green bucket hat and slightly bowed his head in a gesture of high respect.

Hannibal was similar to a human in body characteristics but muscular and MUCH hairier. He wasn't very tall, only about a third of the size of an adult human.

An enthralled Duncan took a more detailed look at Hannibal. With his bucket hat removed, thick, dark, wavy, hair was revealed. Below this there was a faint, diagonal scar above his left eye then very bushy eyebrows and intense-looking dark brown eyes. A dark goatee beard, a gold-capped tooth and a small, shiny, diamond stud earring, completed the Haggi's facial appearance.

He wore a multi-coloured tartan kilt, down to about knee level. The tartan pattern had six colours in it. A dark green base, overlaid in secondary blue squares with subtle lines of white. There were further thinner black and yellow threads then a few more prominent lines in red.

The kilt was held up by a chunky belt with a fancy silver buckle. A sporran hung down at the front.

Duncan wasn't sure what the footwear was but they resembled walking boots and had the same pattern and colouring as the kilt. A small glint of metal was visible from the upper outside of both boots. No socks were worn, so chunky, hairy legs were visible between the bottom of the kilt and the top of the boots.

Hannibal's look was completed by a simple, plain, dark green polo shirt.

To Duncan, the overall appearance of the mythical Haggi was quite comical, rather than scary or threatening.

Duncan's wee visitor's inquisitive eyes flitted about checking for any danger. Hannibal then started talking again, in Jockanese, the language of the Haggi.

"Ma name's Hannibal, Hannibal Bisset, fae the Clan Bisset. Ma maw is frae Clan Anderson. Baith faimily crests contain the mighty oak 'n' be shair that we'll stand oor grund 'n' bounce back in adversity, per the clan mottos."

He continued. "Ah'm cried Hannibal, coz Ah'm the leader ay the Haggi A Team. *That's a wee joke from way before yer time, laddie.* Ah'm pleased tae meet yae, Duncan," said the newcomer, extending his muscular, hairy arm a good yard forward, to shake his hand.

Holy crap, it didn't move its body at all but literally extended its arm towards me.

Haggi Hannibal picked up on Duncan's stunned surprise and said, "Ah kin see yer a smidge freaked oot but the Haggi huv many wee foibles. Like being able to extend 'n' retract oor airms 'n' legs… within reason. This helps us tae easily move up, doon or roond slopes 'n' reach things, withoot needin' oany kit… although Ah ayeways cairry ma twae faithful blades."

Hannibal rotated and extended his arms downwards to demonstrate, lifting a Swiss Army Knife out from his left boot.

Duncan was still too dumbstruck to speak. He was, however, instantly drawn to a capital H on the underside of

Hannibal's left arm, just above the wrist. Pointing at it, he somehow managed to stammer, "That's the same H mark as on the graveyard bench!"

"Aye, laddie, it wiz me thit scratched it oot as a sign fir ye, eftir yir Grandad Hamish tipped us off. Ah crafted that H wi' ma wee dirk. Dirk's an auld Scots word fir a dagger or knife."

He dropped his arm down, lifted the silver blade out of his right boot and briefly showed it to Duncan, then put the dirk back.

"The H is yased as a kind o' secret code. Let me explain. This H oan ma airm is a *Haggoo*. It's a badge ay honour but only fir qualified Haggi warriors. It's like a combined ID, smart card 'n' barcode but huz other powers, like GPS navigation. Helps us tae move aboot 'n' find places withoot gettin' lost. Pretty cool, ye reckon?"

Duncan spoke for the second time to a 'live' Haggi. "Wow, what other stuff can you do?"

"Well, fir starters, we kin mak oorsels invisible, using magic water fae that wee burn there… long story. Plus loadsae other stuff… but… that's aw fir another day… Noo tell me aboot yir troubles at school."

Duncan didn't really know where to start, as he dreaded school and had lots of demons to deal with there. He decided to state the obvious and said, "I really don't like school and wouldn't go if it was up to me. I'd rather just be outdoors and wander free rather than being cooped up like a chicken."

"There must be specific things thit bug ye 'n' mak ye unhappy?" Hannibal prompted.

"Like what?"

"Other pupils, teachers… ye not understanding things that they're trying tae teach ye… aw sorts ay stuff."

"Well, I don't fit in very well. If it wasn't for Davy, I wouldn't have a single pal. We get bullied and shunned for being 'weird' and liking unusual things rather than being into music, sports, and cool stuff like that. Loud noises always hurts my ears, like when the school bell rings or a siren goes off, those type of shrieky things. I get called a lot of names like 'Skinny Malinky' (as in Long Legs)... High Tower... Daftie Dunc... Beanpole... and God knows what else behind my back."

Duncan thought things over for a moment or two then continued. "I sometimes find it hard to read the board and other stuff in class. Plus I already know loads of the stuff we get taught, so I'm really bored half the time and don't get stretched to learn new things. I just switch off. Our teacher Ms Robinson doesn't seem to care or try to check anything, let alone help."

Duncan was finding talking to Hannibal quite therapeutic, and way easier than normal conversations with others, so he pressed on. "Ms Robinson doesn't think we know but she drinks alcohol on the sly at school. Our class call her Ribena. She thinks it's because it rhymes with her name Rowena and her surname is Robinson, like the diluting juice. It's not though, as we know she's got bottles of red wine in her bag and desk. It's the colour of diluted Ribena, so that's why it's her nickname.

"And one final thing... that's not directly to do with me. It's my sister, Mary. She's almost thirteen but still quite naïve, despite having ideas way beyond her years. As she's really pretty and cool, Mary thinks she's the bees knees and attracts quite a bit of attention from the boys. There's an older boy called Brad Thomas and he seemingly has designs on Mary. They're supposed to be going out together on Friday. I think this could go very badly for her, so can you keep an eye on this, please?"

Hagga, hagga… There's plenty to deal with here. "Dae yir maw or da' ken aboot aw this bad stuff at school?"

"No… My dad isn't around anymore. He left about a year ago to go with another woman and we only see him occasionally, at weekends. I'm certainly not going to tell my mum about my school hassles or Mary's love life as I know she's struggling with my dad doing a bunk, plus trying to keep the house going and… fit in her work too. I just don't know what to say or do to try and help her."

Holy guacamole, this kid is having it tough and he's such a lovely laddie. Haggi help is coming his way.

"Listen, Duncan, yir Grandad Hamish wiz a muckle help tae the Haggi 'n' we want tae repay um by helpin' ye, as yir Connected noo. Ah kin tell yiv goat some bad stuff goin' oan but it's gonnae get better, Ah promise ye. The Haggi use stealth, savvy 'n' surprise tae mak things better. We only resort tae aggression as a last resort, but ye dinnae want tae mess wi' a roosed Haggi. There's way mair thin jist me comin' tae yir aid, yil huv a fair wee gang helpin' oot, so dinnae be surprised if other Haggi get in touch wi' ye. I'm gonnae head aff noo, dae ye want tae ask oanythin?"

Duncan was a bit bemused but was on the ball enough to ask, "How do I get in touch with you or other Haggi, from now on?"

"Well, ye can try to get me here or at the graveyard but ye huv tae be careful if non-Connected folks ur aroond. We cannae get compromised." Hannibal continued, "If ye cannae meet up, why don't ye jist sketch stuff or leave messages on yer drawing pad? Leave it in yir room, wi' the windae aff the latch. We kin get in when the hoose is empty during the day."

"OK, I can do that... Sounds like a plan. Thanks, Hannibal."

"Nae wurries, laddie, take care, Ah'll be seeing' ye," were Hannibal's last words.

As Hannibal got ready to leave, he put his green bucket hat back on his head and Duncan noticed two words written, in white, on the front of the hat. He'd originally been too distracted to notice the letters, which spelled out **Stand Sure**.

Hannibal then winked at Duncan and turned to head off, revealing further white characters on the back of the hat. *Tornadoes 0-7 GDIH*.

Duncan's new Haggi pal scuttled away and disappeared from view behind the gorse bushes, to report back to Haggi HQ that connection had been made. Duncan let out a huge exhale and continued to stare where the Haggi had been, still a bit shell shocked by what had just happened. He eventually slumped back down into his grassy den, lay flat on his back and stared up at the light blue sky.

His thoughts flicked over to Grandad Hamish, who had brought this new world to his grandson. "Thanks, Grandad. I won't let you down," whispered Duncan as he got to his feet and picked up his fishing rod.

As he exited his 'den' and headed for home, Duncan dropped a couple of twigs into the water and watched them racing each other down the burbling burn. He was hugely excited and energised after the Haggi encounter but there was also a feeling of unease in how he was going to keep his new allies under wraps.

I'm going to have to share this with Davy at some point but best to say nothing to anyone for now.

Chapter 11

When Duncan had gone out for a walk earlier, Cath's friend and work colleague, Jennifer McDermott, had phoned and suggested dropping round to have a quick coffee chat. Jennifer was worried about Cath as she'd seemed under a lot of stress recently and her gains in self-esteem had dropped away.

Jennifer drove into the street and pulled up outside the McPherson house. As she got out of the car, Mary slammed the front door and came storming down the path. She blasted past, without so much as a glance.

Oh, joy. What am I walking into?

Five minutes later Cath and her good friend were standing in the kitchen, with the noise of the boiling kettle rising to a crescendo. Cath was pacing around and frankly, a bit hyper.

Jennifer had a pretty good idea what Cath was going through as she had two teenage daughters of her own. Although, in her case, she had support from a caring husband, who was still very much part of their household.

"If I was being vindictive, I'd say she was a wee bitch but I've been that age, so I'm willing to cut her some slack. She's going through all sorts of hormonal changes, obsessing on boys, using

Mum as the emotional dart board… but that's normal… isn't it?" Without waiting for an answer, Cath continued. "No, this is squarely down to dad of the year, George. He continually lets them down, when he's supposed to make his rare visits, and thinks that money will solve everything. It's all about his wonderful business, fancy clients and swanning about with his eye candy, super bitch in tow. Well he doesn't have to deal with the sharp end all day, every day."

Cath had, seemingly, run out of steam so Jennifer spoke, slowly and softly. "It's certainly not easy, Cath. The teen years will be tough but… as you say… we weren't much different at Mary's age. We had our moments. Remember, you told me… about… when you threw your shoe, trying to hit your mum in the head, missed and smashed the window."

The mood lightened a little and they both started to laugh.

"Christ, I'd forgotten about that one. I think that was me going off on one because Mum wouldn't let me go to a party with my pals. If I remember right I think I called her 'a foostie wee witch.' Oh my god… I was Mary."

They both had a further chuckle at the historic mother-daughter feud memory and Jennifer moved closer to her friend and gave her a long hug.

With the kettle boiled and coffees made, they moved through and took a more comfortable seat in the living room. Cath felt like she'd got most of her anger and frustration out already.

They inevitably chatted about work stuff for a bit and then Cath gave Jennifer an opportunity to provide some update on what was going on in her domestic circle. Jennifer chatted for a while and outlined that things were, generally, good with them. "The girls are doing well academically and focused more on studying and exams, rather than boys. Although I'm not sure how much longer that'll be the case," she finished with a smile.

Jennifer then continued. "We've just focused on the girls today. How's Duncan getting on?"

"There's definitely something different about him, but I can't put my finger on it. He spends a lot of time outdoors and at the graveyard, 'speaking to Grandad Hamish' in his words. But that isn't unusual, he always does that. He still does his ritualistic eating things and doesn't care about his appearance… He never has… Still good pals with Davy. He's maybe been a bit more secretive recently and also seems less downbeat than normal, so something's definitely happened.

"Duncan showed me a drawing that he'd sketched recently. It was unreal, Jenn… scarily good… it was like top… professional quality. He's obviously had this fabulous gift for a long time and I'd never even noticed this awesome talent. He said it wasn't a big deal and that I'd more to worry about… but what kind of mother am I, that I had no clue about his art abilities?"

"You're a great mum, Cath, and doing a tough job in trying circumstances. Give yourself a break."

Their coffees had gone cold, mostly undrunk.

Cath had benefitted greatly from the opportunity to vent and was very grateful to Jennifer for giving up her Sunday morning to help her.

"I better get going, Cath, things to do for tonight's dinner."

"OK, Jenn, thanks for the chat, you're a star. See you at work tomorrow."

Jennifer took her cup through to the kitchen and put it on

the draining board. "I'll get the cups, Jenn, and thanks again, much appreciated."

They hugged briefly and Jenn headed out the front door of number twenty-eight.

"Take care."

"You too."

Cath stood at her front door and waved her friend off, as her car made its way down the road.

Chapter 12

After leaving Duncan, Hannibal had switched his custom-made, tartan Hagg-boots into 'sleekit mode'. This 'mode' provided a hover layer of air, which cushioned any sound and also rubbed out any footprints, so the Haggi could travel through snow, mud, etcetera without leaving a trail.

Hagg-boots were a cross between, soft-shell running shoes and protective hiking boots, comfortable yet practical. These specialist boots were made by an elderly but expert Haggi cobbler. He was known only as Fit the Bit, came from the North East of Scotland, and while a bit deaf, was dynamite at his job.

Hagg-boots were Fit the Bit's sole product focus, with the other Haggi clothing designed and made by Busy Lizzie and her hard-working, skilled team.

The boots were so highly customised that if anyone other than the owner tried to put them on, a sizeable electric shock would jolt up through their feet and their hair would turn bright green. In addition, they also had a built-in self-cleaning mechanism so, amazingly, Hagg-boots never got dirty.

And so, with boots in 'sleekit mode', Haggi Hannibal made his way along the burn, till it came close to the estate of large, new-build houses. The hairy Haggi then crossed over the small culvert bridge, left the burn behind and turned for home.

He kept away from paths and walkways to avoid detection and progressed through the fields, keeping close to trees and bushes to provide cover. Hannibal passed one group of suitably clad ramblers but they never saw him, safely blended into the foliage.

When he reached the main road, he hid in an empty bus shelter and doubled checked for both vehicles and people. There was no traffic coming from either direction but an older man was coming towards the bus stop, with his trusty wee Westie dog on a lead.

Please just walk past and don't stop at the bus stop.

Thankfully for Hannibal, the man kept walking past without a backward glance, although his dog gave a wee growl and barked as they passed.

"Quiet, Wolfie, there's nae need fir yer barkin'," the old man said as he tugged the lead to usher his dog onward.

Once the old man and his dog were well away, Hannibal double checked the main road again. He saw it was clear so rushed across and ducked into the adjoining hedgerow. The wee Haggi followed the hedge and drainage ditch for about five hundred yards along the main road, keeping out of view.

He reached the well-worn tarmac of the next traffic junction and turned onto this road, heading northwards, away from the town.

Hannibal remained wary but was OK with walking along the road itself, as he knew the chances of being seen were much reduced here. He was pretty fit but had to start working harder as the ground began to rise steadily up towards

Huntsmen Hill.

While Hannibal walked, he couldn't help but feel for Duncan and what he was going through.

He continued to move steadily, while keeping an eye out for any further danger.

By the time the stone cairn came into view at the top of Huntsmen Hill, Hannibal was relieved and a bit out of puff. He stopped under a low tree branch and took a couple of minutes to get his breath back.

He carefully surveyed the area surrounding the cairn and didn't see or hear anything suspicious. Confident that the coast was clear, Hannibal walked up to the cairn and picked up a small receiver, which was carefully hidden, low down, behind two larger stones.

"Haggi A1 returned tae base, headin' doon shortly," he stated.

"Aw righty, A1, see ye soon," replied 'The Hoover', the Haggi on comms duty.

Hannibal replaced the receiver and made sure it was safely hidden away. It was part of the underground Haggi microphone and speaker system. This allowed them to communicate above and below ground from the multiple call points they had installed.

The Haggi view on mobile phones was well established.
- *Tech needs to be dependable.*
- *Mobile phones are all well and good for humans, in fact, they're usually fixed to them.*
- *You can't trust mobiles or mobile network connections, they're not reliable and the GPS would compromise locations* – NOT AN ACCEPTABLE RISK.

Hannibal then carefully stepped out fifty Hagg paces to

the east of the cairn and ducked through a clump of mature trees. A line of unremarkable, small, grassy hills, with some stones in an arch around the lower sections, came into view.

Hannibal walked in front of the fourth of the five hills and stood still. He then extended his left arm upwards to its maximum length, to swipe his Haggoo on a tiny scanner. As he retracted his arm back to normal length, he stated, "Ah'm standin' here at entrance four, if gid fir ye, release the door." [1]

On completion of Hannibal's request, the hidden mechanical cave door to entrance four, creaked into motion and slowly rolled opened.

"In ye come, A1," said 'The Hoover'.

Hannibal stepped through and, as he looked behind himself, the cave door started to close.

---

[1] There are actually several Haggi entrance doors with different entry phrases. For security reasons, if there is any danger, Haggi go to the middle entrance (number 3) and use the appropriate phrase. This acts as a warning system and the Haggi security process would be activated.

Chapter 13

Having just entered the tunnel network of HHHQ (Huntsmen Hill Headquarters), Hannibal let his eyes adjust. The Haggi fitted easily into the round tunnel, although the smooth-bottomed passageways would be too small for an adult human to walk upright in. Every few yards there were low-density roof lights, which aided vision but were not so bright as to blind anyone.

Once his vision corrected, Hannibal started walking down the long, straight tunnel in front of him. His destination was the Haggi Senior Council area so he could report back on his discussion with Duncan.

After walking for a short time, Hannibal came to the first of the numerous T-junctions that made up the Haggi tunnel network. He knew these passages very well but decided to use the Hagg scanners to plot his way. This would give the admin staff time to alert the Senior Council[2] he was on his way,

---

[2] The Senior Council are the eleven decision makers within the Haggi. They are selected from the various colonies around Scotland and are mainly more experienced Haggi, of both sexes. Seven Senior Council members stay within the Huntsmen Hill complex at any time, so that decisions on important matters can be dealt with quickly. Like the Haggi

where he was, and an estimated time of arrival (ETA). This way the important decision makers would be prepared and in place for his arrival to give his update.

Low on the wall at the T-junction was a simple control panel. Rather than bend down, Hannibal extended his left arm while staying upright at his full height. He then 'swiped' his Haggoo across the control panel.[3]

The panel beeped and Hannibal said, "Haggi A1, destination, Senior Council room."

There was a tiny delay then a green arrow, pointing to the right, lit up on the panel.

Part of the way to the next T-junction, Hannibal could see someone, or something ahead, walking in the same direction he was. The figure stopped then unfolded some kind of step mechanism. As Hannibal got closer, he recognised another Haggi, nicknamed, and almost always called, Sparky. His real name was Ronnie Devlin and he was a wizard with electrics, maintenance and in general building-trade skills. The Sparky nickname came from his expert electrician skills but he was also a lightning-quick, trained Haggi warrior so there was double reason for calling him Sparky.

Sparky was very dark and muscular, plus supremely fit. He had very well-trimmed hair for a Haggi, never wore a hat but regularly wore a white muscle t-shirt, which emphasised his impressive build. Through family links, he wore a tartan kilt in Clan Anderson colours, a light blue base with red, black,

---

warriors, when not on duty, they return to their colonies and a rota is worked so that time off is shared evenly.

[3] These control panels only work for trained Haggi. To non-Haggi, this could rapidly turn into a brain-frazzling maze as there are no obvious markings or signs to indicate the way.

yellow, green and navy overlay threads. On his feet were a two-tone (light blue and cream) pair of designer trainers, rather than Hagg-boots, as he was working inside rather than out on a mission.

"How do, Sparky, whit ur ye up tae?"

"Oh, hi Hannibal, I just did a wee bit o' work oan the control panel back there 'n' Ah've goat a bulb tae replace, jist here."

"Good stuff, nae bother tae a man ay your talent."

"Aye, the panel job wisnae too taxin'," said Sparky, modestly.

Hannibal had a quick lightbulb memory and added, "Oh, I nearly forgot, A4," Sparky's Hagg warrior code name, "well done on winning the Haggi warrior fitness comp last week, very impressive."

"Thanks, H, I like tae keep masel' in shape tae keep the youngsters at bay."

"Good lad, nice tae see ye. I'd better press on. See ye later."

Hannibal left Sparky on his mini ladder, fixing a new lightbulb, and headed off to his meeting. He hadn't gone more than two hundred steps, when he heard a muffled engine sound coming from further down the tunnel. The sound got louder and a bright headlight appeared in the tunnel as a vehicle headed towards him. Hannibal stopped walking and moved a bit into the side to allow, what he expected was a Hagg-mobile, to pass.

The now dazzling headlight of the vehicle disappeared as its driver switched off the engine and jumped down in front of Hannibal. He immediately recognised Sammy 'the Tammie', of the Clan Munro, a fellow Haggi warrior of many years' standing. He hadn't seen Sammy for a while but thought he looked in good nick.

Sammy was of similar height and build to Hannibal but perhaps, even more muscular. He had a dry sense of humour but was a tough cookie, having suffered some bad injuries through the years, and was an ace with mechanical things. His hair was a bit lighter than Hannibal's and it was covered by a plain black Tammie (Tam O'Shanter hat) with a silver eagle embossed into it. The eagle was part of the emblem on the Munro clan crest. On the back of his Tammie, in small white capital letters, it said *LC '72 (2-1)*.

Sammy also wore a plain black polo shirt and a knee-length kilt plus Hagg-boots. Both the kilt and boots were patterned in a modern Munro Culloden tartan, a base of red with yellow and black grid lines.

Sammy smiled, showing big white teeth and bear hugged his comrade Haggi as he said, "Hannibal Biz, how's it hingin'?"

"Aw gid, B4, aw gid. Jist met a new Connector 'n' heading tae report back tae Senior Council," replied Hannibal, using Sammy's code name rather than his real one.

"Glad tae hear it. Ah'm daein' great tae, keeping busy between missions."

Hannibal then decided to play his usual word games to wind his pal up. "Sammy… B4. Is that who you are now?"

"Aye, it is and fine well ye ken that."

"Well if that's richt, then whit wur ye, before ye wur B4?"

Sammy was raging that he fallen into Hannibal's word trap (AGAIN).

"Aw man, ye rip ma knittin' every time wi' this. Why did they huv tae gie me this damn code name?"

"Aw part ay the banter, bud. Good tae see ye. Ah better

git oan 'n' no haud ye up."

"Aye, I guess so, see ye soon ya radge."

Sammy got back onto his Hagg-mobile[4], straddling the seat between the four wheels and headed for the mechanical compound, further on up the tunnel network. As he accelerated away down the tunnel, Sammy waved over his shoulder to Hannibal.

Hannibal laughed to himself as he headed off in the opposite direction, away from B4.

After successfully completing the next T-junction, A1 was getting closer to the central hub of the tunnel network. As he neared the centre, Hannibal came to a small recess in the wall. Above the recess was a complex, colourful graphic, showing a broken globe with new growth coming from it and a rainbow arched over the top. Underneath the graphic were the words, 'Yet my hope is unbroken.'

The emblem and motto related to the Scottish clan, Hope.

To the side of the recess, was a separate picture showing a needle gun and ink pots. This was the domain of Ben Jovial, the current in a long line of Hope clan tattooists, who was responsible for the application of the Haggoo onto Haggi warriors, once they had completed their training.

Hannibal realised that there was no one here at the moment but he still had a flashback to the day he got his own H tattoo. A mix of pride at the accomplishment and the pain of the needle puncturing the skin. He glanced down at the H

---

[4] A Hagg-mobile is similar to a child-sized quad bike but with the same 'sleekit mode' technology as in Hagg boots. If this mode is activated, it mutes the sound of the Hagg-mobile engine and rubs out tyre marks as it goes. Hagg-mobiles also have an internal extendable and folding storage cage, which comes out from the back end, and a tow bar in case they need to use a trailer.

on the inside of his left arm, shuddered at the memory, and pressed on through the tunnel network.

After two more control panel swipes, he arrived at the reception area of the Senior Council. After having announced his intentions and progress all the way down the tunnel system, Hannibal expected to be ushered straight in to see them.

He was wrong and a frustrating wait lay in store as he was asked to take a seat by a clearly officious assistant.

Chapter 14

Well away from Huntsmen Hill, George McPherson, Duncan and Mary's dad, was distractedly driving down the M9 motorway in his year-old, metallic-silver Lexus. Marlene, the woman for whom he'd left his family, was in the passenger seat, her tanned, gym-toned legs stretched out, ending in high-heeled shoes that had cost several hundred pounds. She was carefully reapplying lip gloss and working on her perfectly manicured nails, which were in zero danger of damage from any housework.

George had long since zoned out on Marlene's excited ramblings about high fashion and current trends. Instead, he had been subconsciously replaying the core details of the major design deal he had recently agreed and considering the future possibilities with his mega-wealthy new client.

George came back to reality, just as the motorway dipped down to the speed cameras, near the Newbridge roundabout. He slowed down to stay within the fifty-miles-per-hour speed limit at the cameras, then smoothly accelerated his powerful, top-of-the-range motor up the hill and through the right-bearing road section that connected to the M8.

Marlene had insisted on a visit to the Designer Shopping

Centre in Livingston as she "desperately needed" a new outfit for the upcoming wedding of a friend. George had wanted to go clothes shopping like he wanted a hole in the head. He'd much rather have stayed in and watched sport. The Formula 1 season had recently started and he'd fancied watching the race on his huge smart TV in his man cave, deep in their new mansion or 'love nest', as Marlene called it.

When George had put forward his view on the proposed Designer Outlet trip, Marlene had gone into a major strop, throwing stuff around, screaming and acting like a child. Once she'd eventually calmed down and offered him a 'special massage' later, he'd caved in and agreed to the shopping trip.

A few minutes later, they arrived at the Designer Shopping Centre.

George turned right, off the approach road, and made to head for the pay and display car park. Marlene went all mushy, fluttered her eyelashes and said, "Oh, Georgy-poo, please drop me right at the door, I'd never be able to walk from the car park in these heels."

Oh, really? It'll not stop you tottering round every designer shop for the next three hours, you stupid mare.

Instead of acting on what he'd thought, George just said, "Yes, dear," and drove the short distance to the main doors, beside the bus stops, to let the Princess out. He drew the line at getting out and holding the door open for her.

There are limits.

Marlene manoeuvred herself daintily out of the car, blew George a kiss and clip-clopped through the main door into her idea of heaven.

George deliberately took way longer than necessary to find a parking space, pay, display his ticket on the car windscreen, then walk the short distance into the centre.

An extra few minutes out in the fresh air and away from her nonsense is worth its weight in gold.

As George went through the internal doors, a feeling of dread washed over him, as he had a good idea what lay ahead.

Ninety minutes later, Marlene was admiring herself in a pale lemon-coloured dress, with matching fascinator and heeled sandals. A fawning shop assistant waffled sale-driven nonsense and fluffed around her 'sale commission on legs'. The diva of the hour debated, "I really loved that lavender-coloured outfit in the first shop but this one's lovely too. Mind you, the cream one in the shop down the other side was really smart and a possible too. What do you think, Georgey-poo?"

I think I'm losing the will to live.

George bottled it, again, and said, "I don't have the eye to decide such an important decision, you're much better at choosing clothes than I am."

A further twenty minutes later, George was close to slashing his wrists but ended up offering to buy both the lemon ensemble and the other one from the first shop. The cost was fairly eye watering and his credit card would take a huge hit but George was happy to escape with his sanity, just about, intact.

"Oh, you're my stud, George," Marlene simpered as she registered his double purchase offer.

Another half an hour had passed, the two outfits had been bought, paid for and bagged. George had naively thought that would be that but an assortment of candles and soft furnishings had been added to the day's purchases.

He was now marching back to the Lexus to put the purchases in the boot, before returning inside. Thankfully for

George, the diva had shopped herself out and agreed that it was time to rest and recharge. George had suggested eating in the food area of the shopping centre, as he was damned if he was going to cook once he'd driven home. Marlene had a strong aversion to domestic chores and especially cooking but wasn't shy once bubbly fizz came out of the wine cooler.

As George got back to the restaurant area, the proof of the pudding was right there, as Marlene was tucking into a large glass of Prosecco. He sighed to himself, slid into his seat and started to survey the waiting menu.

"I'll just have a salad, got to watch my figure," ventured Marlene.

George ordered a starter and a main, just for the hell of it.

As George finished up his main course, Marlene was on to Prosecco number three and waxing lyrical about her fab fashion purchases. George McPherson had zoned out once again and was mentally replaying his most recent phone conversations with Cath, about cancelling on the kids, again.

I must have been mad but my bed's made now so I'm going to have to lie in it.

Chapter 15

Further up and round the HHHQ tunnel complex from where he'd met Hannibal, Sammy reached his destination. He stopped his Hagg-mobile outside the mechanical department 'complex', as himself and his co-manager, Punnet, called it. It wasn't so much a complex as a big shed, containing lots of parts and components, plus gas tanks for welding, a wee forklift vehicle and a mechanised pulley system.

Separate from the shed there was a fuelling area, a vehicle-checking ramp/pit, and a garage area for storing the Hagg-mobiles. The mechanical department always seemed to have a weird combined smell of oil, fuel, welding and white spirit.

Connected to the main indoor shed area, there was a small toilet and a sectioned-off eating area with a table and chairs. Hagg-mobiles were brought here to be fuelled, repaired, serviced and stored, with other non-Hagg-mobile mechanical jobs also being undertaken.

The workforce here was just two, Sammy and Punnet, co-managers and floor workers. In saying that, they often worked in conjunction with Sparky or Handy, a logistics Haggi, on infrastructure tasks. The installation of the cave access doors near the cairn, was an example of this.

As Sammy walked through the main door into the shed he was surprised not to see Punnet as he was supposed to meet him here at around this time. Just at that moment, Punnet came through from the 'staff area' and into the main shed.

Punnet, codename B3, was so called, simply because he loved strawberries. Punnet's real name was Archibald (Archie) Somerville but most Haggi didn't know this and he was universally 'cried' Punnet. He came from the same lowland Haggi colony as Sammy and they'd been joined at the hip through school, also starting in the HHHQ academy on the same day. Suffice to say they were good buds.

Punnet walked towards Sammy, wearing a black polo shirt, black beanie hat and black Doc Marten boots. He was a fully trained Haggi warrior and would wear Hagg-boots, with appropriate tartan colouring, if on an external mission. For today though, in the shed, his Docs were the order of the day.

Punnet also wore a kilt, decorated in a Somerville clan, modern tartan. This had a red base with dark green square overlay pattern, then a mix of thinner black, yellow, white and mid-blue threads interspersed.

As Punnet walked forward, his kilt looked a bit squint at the bottom. This was due to the fact that one leg was a bit longer than the other, courtesy of a historic Hagg-mobile accident.

Punnet was a bit thinner than Hannibal and Sammy but wiry and strong.

"Oh there ye ur, ya skiver," opened Sammy.

"Jist through the back, pittin' the kettle oan fir a cuppa, 'n' checkin' oan Jasp," replied Punnet.

Jasp was Jasper, the parrot he had acquired while doing some work over in an African Hagg colony. Sammy had also, separately, done 'missionary work' on the African continent.

"Ah huv tae say, yiv done a grand joab oan that mobile, that motor's purrin' noo. Ah gave it foo gutty up the tunnel 'n' it nivir missed a beat. Sleekit mode workin' like a dream tae. Yi'll mak a great mechanic… yin day," said Sammy, the last comment taking the gloss off his praise for his pal.

"Aye 'n' hell 'il freeze ower *before* yir as gid as me, B4," parried Punnet in response, knowing he'd get a reaction.

"Dinnae u start aw that B4 nonsense, Ah've had ma fill o' that aw'ready wi' Hannibal. Talkin' ay which, I saw Hannibal Biz in the tunnel, oan ma waiy here. He's jist back fae a first encounter wi' a new Connection 'n' wiz headin' tae the Senior Cooncil tae report back. Thur may well be some new missions tae git oor teeth intae."

"Aye, that wid be jist grand, things've bin a bit quiet oan the mission front lately," commented Punnet as they headed through the back for a welcome cuppa.

Meanwhile, back down the tunnel network, things had progressed for Hannibal. The officious door keeper had made him jump through several proverbial hoops, before he was finally ushered into the dome-shaped Senior Council area.

The current Senior Council leader was a cheery female Haggi, with kind eyes and a happy disposition. She was clad mainly in a purple/blue-based tartan in accordance with her clan, Elliot. Fortunately, the present Senior Council leader wasn't big on prosaic procedure or wasting time, so she made some quick introductions and asked Hannibal for his report.

Hannibal moved his vision around the horseshoe and the *eleven* Senior Council members.

There's usually only seven here. Mind you, there haven't been many recent new Connections and certainly none with the importance of Hamish McPherson's family. Hamish is obviously still a major deal with the big wigs.

Hannibal regathered his composure, cleared his throat and started speaking. He provided the full Senior Council gathering with detailed information on his conversation with Duncan, plus his own impression of the young lad asking for their help.

A few questions were raised by the learned Council members and answered by Hannibal. The Senior Council leader then requested that they be given time to consider what had been reported back and to decide on appropriate action(s).

The Senior Council leader from clan Elliot thanked Hannibal for his efforts, advised him they'd let him know the outcome of their deliberations, and dismissed him to go about his day.

Hannibal exited with a polite nod, stared daggers at the officious assistant who'd kept him waiting so long, and headed for his living quarters.

Chapter 16

In a small, stone-built cottage, in a village three miles from Auchterbarn, a person who should be important in Duncan McPherson's life was in a bad state.

Rowena Robinson, Duncan's class teacher, tried to open her eyes. It felt as if her eyelids were made of lead and she struggled to shift them apart.

As her eyes opened up, she squinted as her bedroom was much lighter than she had expected it to be. Her brain and vision were a bit fuzzy and she had no clue what time it was.

She patted the bed beside her and felt empty space.

Definitely alone.

Rowena was sure it wasn't a school day as her alarm screeched loud enough to wake the dead and it had definitely NOT gone off today.

It took her several minutes to get on an even keel, then she slowly inched out of her bed. She pulled on her well-worn and beloved dressing gown, then moved tentatively towards the bathroom. The reflection that bounced back from the mirror was a long way from her finest look. Bloodshot eyes and dark, droopy eyelids that could grace a bloodhound, were a stark comparison to the pale, drawn face underneath.

Rowena emptied her bladder and washed her hands. She then brushed her teeth for a good five minutes, in an attempt to remove the red wine taste from her mouth and the stains from her teeth.

She gingerly made it down the stairs to the lower level and checked the living room clock.

It showed three thirty-five.

Holy moley, it must be afternoon as it's bright daylight outside.

Rowena managed to press the button to put the radio on, while she filled the kettle to make a much-needed coffee. While concocting her caffeine brew, the annoyingly cheery radio presenter confirmed it was Sunday afternoon!

You REALLY need to get a grip on this drinking.

Once she had her coffee mug securely held in both shaking hands, Rowena slumped into her comfy armchair. Her eyes travelled across to two photographs that held pride of place in her living room. One showed a smiling, happy, teenage Rowena Preston (as she was then) on a family holiday with her lovely mum and dad. The other was a beautiful wedding photo of a couple, who obviously adored each other.

Powerful waves of emotion poured over Rowena as her mind flashed back to the days on which those photos were taken. The family holiday picture was taken on a caravan holiday in Ayr on the west coast of Scotland. Rowena was thirteen years old and, remarkably for Scotland in summer, it was a beautiful, blue sky, sunny day. She'd had a great time on that holiday with her parents Jim and Elsie, and other family members who had stayed in the adjoining caravans.

She smiled at the memory of playing on the beach with her cousins, making sand castles and larking around in the chilly, salty sea water with Ailsa Craig, home of the granite for curling stones, looking beautiful in the distance.

They had eaten ice cream and fish and chips and, oh my... those local shows with the slot machines, prize bingo and crazy rides.

Last night's drunken meltdown was brought back into focus as Rowena recalled the mind-bending swirling movements of the Wurlitzer ride and the jolting of the dodgem cars, slamming into each other.

The Prestons had thought they couldn't have children of their own but remarkably they had received the greatest gift ever. When Elsie was almost forty, she gave birth to their only child, Rowena.

Fast forward eleven years from the Ayr holiday and the greatest-gift daughter had graduated from university and completed her teacher training. She took up her first full-time teaching post shortly afterwards, coincidentally in Ayrshire, and her parents were the proudest on the planet. They supported and loved her unconditionally but, in less than five years, they were gone.

Her wonderful parents were removed from her life, courtesy of a horrendous car accident.

Rowena was distraught at their passing and came close to having a total breakdown in the aftermath. With the support of an understanding local doctor, she eventually got herself back on her feet and returned to work, although some of the light had gone out.

Life was pretty hard for a couple of years but Rowena coped by investing heavily in the kids, whom she taught day to day. While they brought their challenges, she loved their youthful enthusiasm and lust for life and learning.

Two weeks before her thirty-second birthday, life turned

for the better and she met a lovely guy called Robbie Robinson. They were introduced through one of Rowena's fellow teachers and she had instantly known that this guy was a keeper. He wasn't the most handsome or the cleverest man but he treated Rowena as if she was the Queen of the World. It didn't take long for her to know that Robbie Robinson was the man for her and they got engaged within six months.

The planning of the big day was detailed and set for a date exactly two years from the day they had met. It was to be held in an intimate rural location, with lovely mature trees overhanging a river, which ran down one side of the small wedding venue. A beautiful stone bridge and farmland was visible from the huge window, near to which they would take their sacred vows.

Rowena's chosen wedding dress was a simple but classy cream colour with subtle and intricate embroidered flowers on it. Her veil, cake and flowers were also simple yet stunning, all chosen with care and attention.

Although her dad would not be there to walk her down the aisle, six months before their wedding, Rowena had been certain everything was going to be perfect.

Except it wasn't.

Four months before their wedding, Robbie went to see his doctor, as he'd been having regular, severe headaches. After a barrage of tests over four weeks the doctor provided devastating news.

"I'm sorry, Mr Robinson, but you have an inoperable brain tumour and have four months, at best."

Undeterred by this horrific news, the loving couple moved the wedding forward a few weeks and married in a simple registry office ceremony. It still meant the world to them both.

The wedding photo in Rowena's living room was taken on that day, the happiest but also one of the saddest in her life. Robbie died, six weeks later, in Rowena's arms.

It wasn't hard to follow that Rowena Robinson had suffered unbearable heartache in her forty-something years.

She pulled her gaze away from the photos and stood up from the armchair. Her eyes were full of heavy tears, as she carried her coffee cup into the kitchen. Her sorrow only deepened as she noticed the four empty bottles of Shiraz, sat on the kitchen worktop.

When Robbie had died, Rowena felt like the world had ended. She had several good friends who had done more than could be expected, however, Rowena had never felt so completely and utterly alone.

Her downward spiral into alcohol had begun then.

It started off with an odd bottle of wine at the weekend.

This moved on to a bottle or two every second night.

The love of the classroom and her pupils drained with each glass that passed her lips.

As the years went by, she did her job, passably, picked up her pay cheque and boosted her pension but her new love had slowly become the contents of a bottle.

On this Sunday afternoon Rowena avoided the temptation to revisit her liquid love. She went upstairs to bed and set her alarm for school in the morning, having enough awareness to remember that the clocks changed last night. She shifted the time by an hour and settled down for the night.

As she had stirred historic memories and reopened old wounds, all the self-doubt and questions resurfaced.

Why me?

Why all this horrendous bad luck?

Am I a jinx?
Do I make these things happen?
Sleep was going to be hard to achieve.

Chapter 17

After being dismissed from the Senior Council, Hannibal was contemplating going towards his Hagg-cave (living quarters) to get some rest.

As he started walking, his stomach rumbled loudly, indicating that food would be a very good idea. He'd been on the go for a long time without eating or drinking anything, so this would need to be remedied. He started to make for the kitchen/canteen area.

After walking for a minute or so along the tunnel, he reached a recessed opening with a trap door set into the floor. It looked like it dropped down into the bowels of the Haggi headquarters. It did, indeed, go WAY down, into a production and storage area, where the Haggi alcohol of choice was made and stored. This was the domain of a Haggi with northern roots, named 'Mental Mac'. This was his name for two reasons.

Firstly, in the old days he was always moving around the Highlands, regularly falling out with people and nobody was sure of his real name or origin.

Secondly, he was always doing crazy/mental things, so 'Mental' stuck as it was alliterative to Mac (which was as good a moniker as any for a Scottish Highlander).

He was rumoured to be from clan MacKinnon as he wore a boar's head (clan emblem) on his clothing and before missions or fights he was alleged to have shouted Fortune Favours The Bold (clan motto). As a younger front line Highlander Haggi warrior, he had more than lived up to this motto and his tough warrior reputation. No situation was off-limits to Mental Mac, he just piled in, not always considering the consequences.

The legend that grew was of a warrior, small in size but huge in attitude and bravery, often against more sizeable opponents. He got involved in hundreds of fights, sometimes justified, sometimes not, and had a very long memory for anyone that crossed him or did him harm. He had handed out plenty 'punishment' over the years but eventually suffered so many concussions, that the Senior Council had retired him from frontline duties.

Wir gonnae huv tae protect um fae hissel'.

He was also a Haggi snow specialist, when still on active service, and was a renowned skier.

Due to his rumoured clan links to the drink trade and years of brave warrior service, he was given the role of chief brewer and protector of the Haggi beverage, Berry Brew.

Hannibal pulled the trap door open and shouted, "Ur ye doon there, Mental?"

"Ah um, whae's askin'?" came the reply from the depths.

"Hannibal, A1."

"Ah'm headin' up."

A head appeared revealing black-rimmed glasses, tucked neatly under bushy, black eyebrows. The glasses, unusual wear for a Haggi, were held in place by a nose that had been broken several times during active service.

Some tidy, grey hair poked out under a predominantly orange-coloured baseball cap. The cap had a boar's head emblem on it.

As Mac pulled himself up out of the hatch, he was a bit out of puff after the long ladder climb. The Haggi now standing before Hannibal was dressed in a tartan kilt (red base with green square overlay and mainly white inlay threads) and a black Lacoste polo shirt. A pair of designer black trainers were on his feet.

As he stepped out into the light of the tunnel, the Berry Brew custodian switched to his prescription sunglasses to shield the light.

"Ah'm yased tae bein' doon there, it's like bein' a miner," he volunteered. "Sod thit fur a job tho'. How's you, A1?"

"Aw gid here, jist reported tae Senior Council eftir a meet wi' a new Connector, a McPherson nae less. Could be some interesting mission time coming up fir us active laddies."

"That sounds jist braw, I'd love tae be in there wi' youse lads. But the codger cooncil dinnae let me loose oanymare, mair's the pity," lamented Mental Mac, pining for being in amongst the action.

"So, G1," Mac's Haggi codename, "whit's keepin' ye busy wi' the Berry Brew?" asked Hannibal.

"Wur tryin' a wee tweak tae the recipe. Keep the same braw flavour but reducing the 'kick' so it reduces the length o' 'sleepy time'. Auld Eddie Wood keeps the flow ay quality fruit coming fae the gairden set up, 'n' maintains the purified water fae the burn. But as ye well ken, the Berry Brew recipe is a highly guarded secret 'n' very few ur in the loop."

"Sounds interesting, Chief, Ah'm shair yi'll crack the recipe change. Better go, I'm Hank Marvin 'n' headin' fir the canteen. See ye aroond."

"Aye A1, catch ye later… 'n' gie any chancers an extra dunt fi' me."

Hannibal gave a brief wave and headed onward through the tunnel network. Mac decided to stay 'top side' so he locked down the Berry Brew tunnel hatch. Due to the highly sought-after product stored below, the hatch was protected by a touchscreen combination mechanism that another Haggi, known as Handy, had devised.

Less than five Haggi knew how to open the hatch, Mac being one of them.

After leaving Mac behind, Hannibal passed one further T-junction control panel and arrived at the kitchen/canteen area.

"Hiya, son, what kin Ah git ye the day?" asked Helen Black, a long-serving member of the Haggi canteen support staff, as Hannibal walked towards the counter. This lady Haggi had a rep for knowing everybody, as she'd been around so long.

"Can Ah please huv a large lentil soup, 'n' two weel-fired rolls wi' plenty butter 'n' whatever's the freshest o' Nessie's jams. Ah'll jist eat them here, as Ah'm ravenous."

Nessie was a more mature kitchen worker, who made amazing soups and jams. She was also a very clever Haggi and was the 'go to' for any queries about Haggi history.

As Hannibal made his food order, Helen didn't react at all and just gave Hannibal a strange wee smile. He wasn't sure what was going on, then remembered that she was somewhat deaf, more so on one side, even with her hearing aids in. He moved round towards her 'good' ear and repeated his order.

"Aw right, got ye noo, laddie," said the veteran server as she disappeared behind the screen to get his order.

Helen soon returned with Hannibal's food. He thanked her, got a spoon from the cutlery section for his soup, and took a seat at the dining table behind him to satisfy his hunger.

Given how hungry he was, Hannibal finished his soup and jam rolls in rapid time. He licked his lips, savouring the taste as he finished, then set off with renewed energy back to his Hagg-cave.

"Lovely grub. Catch ye soon, ladies," called Hannibal.

Helen replied, "Yes, dear."

Between the canteen and his living quarters, Hannibal knew that he'd have to pass the Haggi training area for new recruits. As he got a little nearer, he could hear faint chanting. The sound got louder as he got closer.

Hannibal couldn't see the source but he could, however, make out the familiar voice of Drill Sergeant Norrie Gordon. He was issuing commands to his charges, who were practicing their marching and singing a Haggi song, as they did so.

We are the Haggi warriors, We come from hill and glen.
Search fir badness, sort it oot, Then head back hame again.

The song brought a wee smile to Hannibal's face as he thought about the Haggi adventures he'd been on and the camaraderie that came with it. They did enjoy their wee sing-songs on their travels, when there were no humans around to hear them.

The other thing they liked (a lot) was Berry Brew, the alcoholic drink made from wild fruits, using a secret Haggi recipe. It was no wonder that Mental Mac had to guard the Berry Brew and was trying to dilute its potency. The Brew was massively popular as it had fabulous flavour and made you feel fantastic BUT even a smallish amount led to hours and hours of comatose slumber.

As it was vital to have Haggi warriors alert and ready for missions at all times, Senior Council had introduced heavy controls and rationing. Accordingly, Berry Brew was only issued for specific external missions, on special celebrations or in minute doses, to aid insomnia.

His subconscious brought the connected rhyme to the forefront:

Ayeways respect the Berry Brew
'N' the buzz, which it, can gie, tae you,
But shut yir eyes 'n' it's got yir number,
Inducin' hours of knocked oot slumber.

Hannibal walked on beyond the drill ground without stopping, smiling widely as he went.

Chapter 18

After all his travels and encounters over the last few hours, A1 was relieved to be at his 'digs' at last. He felt pretty tired out as he opened the door of the Hagg-cave, which he shared with another Haggi.

In front of Hannibal was a nicely set-up living pod. There was a central seating area with a table and four chairs; a small kitchen with a cooking hob, microwave and sink; a bathroom, including a toilet and power shower; and two bedrooms, off to either side.

The bedrooms both had a high-powered blow drier fitted into the ceiling. This was required as wet Haggi hair took A LOT of drying out.

Hannibal had a cave mate but the first person he saw wasn't his roomie, but instead a Haggi nicknamed Steely. Kai 'Steely' Steel (codename A2) was one of the younger, fully trained Haggi warriors. Like many Haggi he multitasked and used his flooring and DIY skills to keep the HHHQ facilities in good order. Steely was on the floor in the back left corner of the living area, finishing off a replacement floor section.

When he heard the door open, Steely turned his head to see who was there.

As Hannibal walked in, he recognised Steely and relaxed, also noticing the green lettering *YLT – GGTTH* on the back of Steely's white work polo shirt.

"Oh, it's you, Steely, ye look like yiv nearly finished. That's a gid job yiv done," complimented Hannibal.

"Aye that wiz the last wee section, Ah'm done," replied Steely as he got off his knees, took off his knee pads and turned, facing into the Hagg-cave.

Steely had dark, tanned skin and was tall and long limbed for a Haggi. He regularly worked out and was deceptively strong with excellent hand-to-hand fighting skills. He was wearing black cargo trousers rather than a kilt, which he only wore on an occasional mission. The cargo trouser pockets were handy for tools when doing DIY, so were more practical than a kilt.

On the front of his white polo shirt was a square block of Anderson tartan (via clan links) with the words *Stand Sure A2* (his warrior codename).

Soft material comfy trainers completed Steely's working attire as they were lightweight and flexible.

Hannibal was visibly flagging. He stretched, yawned loudly and wandered through to his bedroom area. Steely took the hint and left, shouting out to Hannibal, "That's me done, A1, Ah'm off, Ah'l catch ye later."

The door had barely closed when it opened again. This time it was Hannibal's cave buddy. In walked Gordon 'Handy' Greig, codename (C1), a very patriotic Haggi. He often wore a dark blue polo shirt to match the national team colours and allied this with a kilt in the dark shades of red and green of the noble Greig clan tartan. He also wore Hagg-boots in the clan colours and a dark blue baseball cap with the inscription *2016 (3-2), SDG 90+ 2*, in white letters.

Gordon (AKA Handy) was a tall, solid, experienced Haggi warrior but these days only went into the field on rare occasions. There weren't all that many missions these days and he had a lot of things to supervise. He wasn't as quick as he'd been in his footballing days so was happy to leave the live-action stuff to the younger bucks, these days.

Handy's nickname arose from his Haggi job title, PALM (Premises And Logistics Manager), allied to being really handy at multiple disciplines. Where there was technical, equipment or building requirements around HHHQ or on missions in the field, Handy would be involved. Amongst many other things Handy had been heavily involved in designing and overseeing the installation of the HHHQ access doors and tunnel control panels. A lesser engineering feat but highly important project, was his work in co-designing the Special Water apparatus, enabling Haggi invisibility.

Handy coordinated with Sammy and Punnet (mechanical), Sparky (electrics) and to a lesser extent Steely and Strummer (in-house decor). This way he had a good handle on things and could then provide updates on behalf of a much wider group to save multiple meetings. The others could therefore be in the field, while Handy handled the internal management.

Big Tony, the Haggi tech guru (video, audio, some communications and programming) had badly injured his knees on a mission a while back, so was no longer an active warrior. He had been interested in 'techy' things before his injuries, so had been moved into specialising in this area.

Big Tony was codenamed E2 and a cousin of Hannibal, so wore Bisset clan colours, if the occasion required. He often wore a white baseball cap with *1991 LC - Ted* in green letters.

E2 worked solo on his tech stuff with occasional input on computer code from Auntie, another in-house Haggi worker.

Big Tony also reported to Handy, rather than attending meetings personally, so that the tech area was manned as often as possible.

Back in his Hagg-cave, Hannibal had sat down on his bed and after some groaning and heaving, had got his Hagg-boots off.

There was silence for about thirty seconds.

"Whit's that pong?" enquired Handy, as his smelling senses went into overload.

"Ah jist took ma Hagg-boots aff, ya cheeky git," replied an ever more tired Hannibal.

"Oh, ya minger, yir feet ur honkin' worse than that veiny blue cheese," said a disgusted Handy.

"Well dinnae ask me fur oany, next time ye want some toppin' fur yer crackers," was Hannibal's retort.

"Oh, Ah'm gonnae boak. That's rancid, man," answered Handy as he shut his bedroom door to try to escape the awful smell.

Handy waited in his room for ten minutes to let the 'blue cheese' odour disappear. As he walked back into the main living area he could hear load snoring coming from Hannibal's room.

"My god, man, nae jist rancid trotters… yer snorin' like a piston in a tunnel."

"Pot, kettle, black, ya radge, yiv woken me up again, gie it a rest."

Handy didn't reply, keeping his powder dry for another time.

As Hannibal felt himself begin to nod off, he remembered

that after a nap, he needed to check on the doos later.

Mental Mac shared a Hagg-cave with a 'still active' Haggi warrior called Strummer. Their cave was at the opposite end of the accommodation section from Hannibal and Handy.

When Mental Mac had locked up the Berry Brew hatch and headed for home, he thought it would be quieter, with it being a Sunday in HHHQ.

Unfortunately for him, he was wrong.

Firstly, Drill Sgt Norrie Gordon had come out of the drill parade area, just as Mac was passing. He unwittingly got dragged into a lengthy discussion about the glory days and multiple missions. This was then compounded by Helen Black arriving on the scene, after her canteen shift, and adding to the memory mix.

"…Ye definitely ken thum, son…" Helen rounded out insistently, describing several Haggi that Mac most certainly did NOT know.

G1 eventually extricated himself, hopefully without any offence to his elders, and had no further encounters on his way home.

As Mac reached 'home' and opened the door of his 'digs' he could hear singing coming from the other bedroom, which wasn't his. This was no doubt his room-mate Strummer, trying out some new lyrics for his latest song.

Just as Mac shouted to let his buddy know he was 'home', an industrial-strength hair drier went on. The deafening noise continued for what seemed a very long time. Then, thankfully, it stopped.

Strummer appeared in the doorway, looking like a giant fur ball, with a towel wrapped round his waist. He jumped back in fright when he saw Mental Mac sitting in the living area.

"Christ, man, Ah didnae ken ye wir there," said Strummer.

"Ah did shout, when Ah came in."

"Didnae hear a thing."

"Nae wonder, ye'd huv to huv lugs like an African elephant, tae even huv a chance ay hearin' o'er that drier."

"True. I'd spilt a paint pot oan a job 'n' hud tae shower fur ages tae try tae git aw the paint aff ma fur. Then yase the wind tunnel tae get it dry."

As well as a highly effective warrior, Strummer multitasked as a painting and decorating specialist, hence his paint issue.

Mac was struggling to stifle laughter at Strummer's huge bouffant hair and eventually said, "Ye look like a poodle in Crufts, aw ye need is the fancy clippin' roond the edges."

"Gies peace, ya muppet, yer jist jealous o' ma hirsute Haggi-ness."

They both then cracked up laughing.

Strummer's code name was D1 and his formal name was James Stoddart the 5th. This may seem like a lot of James Stoddarts, but this Scottish border area surname, meaning breeder of horses, goes back many centuries. As with many warriors, no one used his real name and he was universally known as Strummer. He generally wore black polo shirts and cargo trousers for HHHQ activities but wore a kilt in the blue-based tartan of Clark's Harbour, Nova Scotia, when in the field, as this was designed by a fellow Stoddart.

He loved all things music, often jammed on his wee Hagg guitar or drum kit and had liked the band The Clash, back in the day. Their singer and founder member was called Joe Strummer and hence his nickname had been established.

The Haggi Strummer had a tough upbringing in an area where any weakness would be exploited, but he hadn't been found wanting very often and wasn't someone to be messed with. In saying that, he was very much the joker in the Haggi pack and always had jokes to tell, plus banter galore.

Strummer was of average height but with huge arms like anvils and a body like a tree trunk. D1 was fiercely loyal to those dear to him and would never stand back when action was required.

Mental Mac liked having Strummer as his room-mate as they always had great banter. Mac also got to hear about present-day missions as he missed the close-quarters work, out in the big world.

Chapter 19

After Hannibal had briefed them, the Haggi Senior Council had deliberated and made their decision. They unanimously agreed that, starting from early tomorrow (Monday):-

1. A small Haggi reconnaissance squad would visit the school and check out what Duncan had told Hannibal about the bullies and his teacher.

2. Another small reconnaissance squad would be shadowing Brad Thomas to check his activities and make sure no harm came to Mary.

Hannibal had firmly communicated that he believed what Duncan had told him but it was always Haggi best practice to check things out themselves. They could then make plans of action from a position of knowledge.

The Senior Council decision was posted on the comms system and Hannibal informed directly by a messenger, so he could organise the separate teams for the next day.

*

Down in Auchterbarn Town Hall, another big decision had been made.

The Gala Week Organising Committee had agreed that

this year's Gala Queen was to be Steph Findlay.

The vote for their pupil 'Queen' had been very close. With input from residents and their own views to consider, the committee had debated long and hard. In the end, Mary McPherson had narrowly lost out to her best friend. To soften the blow for Mary, the committee had agreed to create a role of Best Maid to the Queen. They weren't sure if Mary would even accept this secondary role but hoped she'd be mature enough to agree, rather than miss out on the Gala Parade altogether.

The Committee congratulated themselves on a job well done and they continued with their planning for the town's big summer event.

The Glam Gang didn't meet up at the weekend after their big drama fallout at school on Friday. Each of the four girls did normal routine weekend activities with or without their families. They were blissfully unaware of the Gala Week Committee decision.

They were also totally unaware that they were all being watched and it had nothing to do with the Haggi.

Chapter 20

As the Senior Council had sanctioned, Haggi warriors were to go to Auchterbarn Primary School on Monday morning. Their role was to observe the school but with a clear focus on the behaviour of the alleged bullies and Duncan's teacher, Ms Robinson.

Hannibal (A1), Strummer (D1), and Sparky (A4) were dispatched and eager to get started on checking what Duncan had told them. From even limited observation pre-school and at break time, the Haggi had absolutely no doubt. The Burgan twins were exactly what Duncan had said – unashamed, straight-up bullies. Rather than refer back to Senior Council, Hannibal spoke to Strummer and Sparky and they unanimously agreed that action was going to happen sooner, rather than later.

"These bullies huv it comin' tae thum, Ah'm gonnae enjoy this wee scrap," said Sparky, itching for action.

"Remember, lads, we cannae jist sort it oorsels. We need Duncan involved tae boost his confidence 'n' avoid compromisin' the Haggi. Timin'll be key, wait fur ma say-so, before any fisty cuffs, richt?" cautioned Hannibal.

Sparky and Strummer nodded their agreement but

harboured their own thoughts about revenge on the bullies.

Wee scrotes ur gettin a dooin'.

*

It was Monday morning, underground in the Huntsmen Hill, Headquarters (HHHQ). Various Haggi warriors were away, carrying out their surveillance at the primary school and further afield. Meanwhile, the hugely important, non-field operations in HHHQ were in full flow.

All of the key staff were working today, most having travelled in from external Haggi colonies, after enjoying the weekend with their families.

The Haggi were renowned for their ability to have a mix of skills and to multi-task.

There was a real buzz of activity and gossip in the air, as word of a new Connection spread like wildfire. The fact that several warriors had been dispatched 'Doon the Toon' on fact-finding missions backed up the new Connection rumour.

A tall, female Haggi was doing the rounds, checking in with everyone to make sure that all actions were in hand and nothing dropped through the cracks. She was dressed very smartly in comfortable, business-casual clothing with the words *Stand Sure* subtly imprinted on both sleeves of her white blouse. Her name was Martha McMillan (importantly Mc not Mac) but the Haggi simply called her 'The Boss' and she was the unofficial chief operating officer/social convenor of HHHQ.

The Boss was very adept at keeping all the proverbial Haggi plates spinning and kept people onboard through her caring and supportive nature. That was not to be confused with someone who was an easy touch. The Boss would always praise, where it was justified, but set high standards for herself and others, as well as being assertive and speaking her mind freely. Great as an ally but if you went to the dark side, the 'stink eye' would follow and plenty of making up would be required to get back on-side.

Although not a Haggi warrior, The Boss did lots of fitness classes and was in excellent shape.

Handy had already dropped by the central admin office and spoken to The Boss, to provide his updates for PALM, mechanical, electrical, tech and décor sections.

The colourful, comfy Hagg-boots on The Boss's feet were now making their way along a central Haggi tunnel. In the distance she could hear a loud, distinctive laugh plus... singing.

The Boss smiled and chuckled as realisation hit, of where she was in the Haggi underground network. As she got closer, she could hear the words of the song more clearly:

"...young and sweet, only seventeen..."

It's Lindy, the Dancing Queen.

As she got to the door of Lindy's domain it was an interesting spectacle, to say the least. Lindy, AKA the Dancing Queen, was a part of Clan Hope and a relative of Ben Jovial, the Haggoo tattooist. She always wore something with a rainbow on it to account for the rainbow on the clan crest. Today, the Dancing Queen was wearing a rainbow-coloured jumper, with her trademark hair in side bunches. Today's hair colour was bright red.

A pair of denim jeans were fairly subdued in comparison but offset by a pair of Hagg-boots in the Hope tartan colours (predominantly darker green and blue with yellow and black threads).

Lindy, typical of Haggi multi-tasking, did three jobs during her working week, namely hairdressing, chemist dispenser, and bed linen laundry. Today was combined between Haggi hairdressing and operating the small dispensary.

Twice a week, she helped out with the bed linen. The Haggi warriors got their bedclothes laundered for them but had to do all their other washing themselves, in the communal laundry.

"Hi, Lindy, yir looking colourful the day, how's it goin?" said The Boss.

"Excellent, ta. This mornin' Ah've done a couple o' wee beard trims for lassie trainees[5] 'n' given oot three or four packs o' anti-moggie tabs."[6]

"Great stuff. Incidentally, is thir much demand fir Berry Brew fir insomnia these days?"

"No' really, loadsae folk yased tae be 'at it' before but hardly oany these days."

"OK, Lindy, keep up the gid work, catch ye fur the karaoke oan Thursday eftir work. Bring yer microphone… See ye."

The Boss smiled as Lindy went back into song mode, then carried on her rounds and went to the central communication area.

"Morning, Heather. Whit's happening?" opened The Boss.

"Nae much oot the ordinary, jist sortin' the monthly newsletter wordin'," said Heather, AKA The Hoover.

She had this moniker for two reasons. Firstly, her surname was Henry, so some thought the Hoover brand reference was amusing. Secondly, Heather had the ability to hoover up information and skilfully use it in a number of ways.

Her primary role was the Haggi communications

---

[5] All Haggi are very hairy. Even children and women have facial hair, some opting for a goatee and/or moustache look.
[6] ALL Haggi are allergic to cats so regularly take antihistamine medicines to help.

controller, which had its challenges, as the Haggi never used mobiles or tablets with GPS tracking capability, to protect their locations. Therefore communications via more modern tech were done on the Hagg-net, an internal electronic reference and communication system with its own inbuilt, untraceable circuitry and connection. This was used for keeping the younger and more tech-savvy Haggi and overseas colonies (e.g. Haggaroos in Australia), updated on events such as important news, security measures, upcoming missions or Senior Council rulings.

In addition, foreign-language versions were provided for the Hagg clans overseas, who had another 'first' language, such as Los Haggaleros (in Spain and Mexico).

There was an occasional need to handle physical HHHQ entry comms for Haggi gaining access to the tunnel network but this was only one weekend in four, to cover shifts.

Heather was generally quiet and not flamboyant, so didn't adopt any bright clan colours. She was very studious, organised, a team player, calm and patient under pressure.

Another part of her role was to co-ordinate messages to Haggi 'oldies', who weren't tech savvy and preferred communication on paper. Heather would compose the message, which would then be handwritten by Elsie Brunton, a Haggi famous for her beautiful handwriting.

The messages were then sent via pigeons, trained by Hannibal, for delivering to the Scottish Haggi colonies. Heather particularly loved compiling the Gaelic version for the Haggi in remote Scottish communities and this was what she was currently working on.

"Sounds like yer daein' an ace job as usual. Keep it up 'n' dinnae forget it's the monthly quiz next week. Wur defending champs, so git swattin'," said The Boss, as she left Heather to her Gaelic compilation.

The Boss walked quietly for a few minutes, till she could hear sounds of exertion coming from the training grounds. As the tunnel opened out onto the wider training area, she could see the Haggi warrior trainees being put through their paces by a female Haggi.

Elsie Brunton was tall, held her posture very well, and was running today's training session. She'd been an excellent all-round athlete in her younger years, so now assisted in training new recruits. Elsie was also a very good swimmer, so covered a lot of the 'in water' training, often in the purified Auchterbarn burn area.

There had been quite a shift in Haggi warrior recruitment in more recent times and The Boss noted several female trainees within the larger group. There were also a few dark-skinned Haggi within the training squad. She knew from previous discussions that the trainees were the children of African Haggi, whom Sammy and Punnet had worked with overseas.

The trainee group were currently working on limb extension and flexibility practice, on an elaborate climbing frame and a variety of other objects.

The Boss waved to Elsie in the distance and headed into the training centre structure. Within the training admin office, sat a very grumpy-looking female Haggi.

"Hi, Lulu, you look like you're luvin' yer job this mornin'," opened The Boss.

"Updatin' trainee progress reports, is'nae ma idea o' fun. I'd much rather be oot there, training thum, than stuck in here daein' paperwork," replied Lulu, stating her position on things.

Lulu (code name A3, AKA ICU) stood up from the desk and stretched her arms upwards. "That's better, gettin' some blood runnin'," she said, her mood improving.

She had long legs and was even taller than The Boss.

Lulu was dressed simply in black gym gear, befitting her role as an extremely fit Haggi warrior and the head training instructor. Her dark hair today was in a long ponytail, held by a green and white scrunchy. The black Newsboy hat that was sitting on her desk had *Stand Sure A3* written on the front in white. There were white characters on the back of the hat too – *SoL '07 (5-1)*.

Lulu was a striking Haggi anyway but she had one very prominent feature, namely one bright copper-coloured eye, to accompany her other dark brown one.

This was where her nickname of ICU came from.

Eye (of) Copper. Eye = I. Cu – chemical symbol for copper.

Lulu had proved to be one of the highest performing trainees EVER. After becoming a fully-fledged Haggi warrior and excelling on missions, The Boss and Senior Council had given her the role of Head of Recruit Training.

They knew that male Haggi were likely to expect a male trainer and underestimate Lulu. Several trainees had done exactly this, to their cost, and had nursed the bruises to their bodies and egos as a result.

Lulu/ICU was a great training instructor but boy, did she hate the related admin reports.

"How ur oor latest group progressing?" asked The Boss.

"Thir aw daein' well but the African Haggi ur pretty impressive. I'd think that with additional hand-tae-hand combat and field training, this whole group should be ready for stepping up within a month or twae."

"That's excellent, Lulu. Fancy a cuppa?"

"Aye, that'll break up this crappy paperwork."

As the kettle was boiling and the mugs being looked out, a new visitor arrived.

"Mornin' all, Ah've jist dropped in tae chat tae Lulu aboot trainee support," said Jean Gordon, AKA Auntie.

'Auntie' was another highly skilled all-rounder. She was blonde-haired and dressed in her standard Gordon dress tartan skirt and plain white blouse.

Always available, making sure everyone was OK and passing on hints, tips and guidance as required, she covered multiple roles including trainee welfare. As an excellent cook, she worked in and supervised the kitchen/canteen department, with Nessie as support as the soup and jam guru. Also adept at making things and handy on a sewing machine, Auntie made items and oversaw operations in the clothing department, while giving Lizzie her place as the head honcho. And just to round things off, Jean was a computer whiz, so occasionally helped tech guru Big Tony, with system issues or complex code.

The door had barely closed behind Jean, when there was a knock and another visitor popped her head round the door. "Hi, ladies. Ah wiz jist passin' 'n' saw Jean drop in, so headed in tae, as Ah wanted a wee chat wi' her aboot kitchen supplies," added Lorraine Driver, AKA the Sourceror, as she was a wizard at externally sourcing all Haggi requirements.

LD the Sourceror was tall and slim with long dark hair. She was well turned out as always in light-coloured, smart but casual clothes. Discreetly embroidered onto both sleeves of her white blouse was the inscription – *Stand Sure, Q&O*.

"Come on in, sit yirsels doon, kettle's oan," said The Boss.

The other three sat down, while the Boss sorted the teas and coffees. Lulu was delighted to be away from report cards and have some different chat.

"Whit wiz it ye wanted tae ask me?" asked Jean, of the Sourceror.

"Whit wis it again? Oh aye, dae ye need oany utensils or equipment fur the kitchen or canteen?"

"Naw, Ah dinnae think so, we dinnae yase oanythin' very fancy, jist the old-fashioned waiys. It's ayeways intrigued me though, how whit we order, jist seems tae appear, as if by magic. How dae you dae it?"

"Normally, Ah'd say that if Ah telt ye, Ah'd huv tae kill ye," LD jokily started to reply, then delayed, waiting for a reaction.

Auntie's face looked like she believed it for a second, then she sussed the ruse and smiled.

The master of procurement continued, "But, since yir in wi' the bricks, Ah'll let ye in oan the secret. As ye ken, tae avoid detection or the HHHQ being compromised, the Haggi dinnae yase oany devices thit kin be GPS tracked. Thit doesnae mean such devices cannae be yased elsewhere though.

"Thir ur a few connected families in other toons, a bit away fae Auchterbarn. As we've helped them oot in the past, Ah go tae their hooses 'n' yase their mobiles, iPads or Android devices 'n' credit cards tae impersonate a human. Ah dae online shopping orders fae supermarkets fur home delivery 'n' online shop fir bigger items. We square thum up fur the cost 'n' awthin' is delivered tae Connectors' addresses so thit HHHQ is nivir mentioned oanywhere.

"Then we huv tae transport the stuff. Masel 'n' Heather

coordinate Haggi warriors 'n' trainees tae dae the pick-ups oan Hagg-mobiles at night. They bring the stuff back tae HHHQ 'n' when ye arrive at the kitchen in the mornin', voila… supplies ur aw in place."

"Wow, that's ingenious. Must tak some organisin', aw that?" said a very impressed Jean.

"It's jist what Ah dae. Nae bother really," replied LD modestly.

The Boss handed out the beverages and put some biscuits out on a plate.

The conversation continued.

"So, girls, how's things in clothing wi' Lizzie?" asked The Boss.

As LD was very clued up on fashion and helped out in the clothing area, she kicked off the response. "Interestin' 'n' challengin'. Lizzie's the best wi' a needle 'n' thread 'n' huz dun stitchin' oan fabric, humans and animals alike. She's a great auld girl bit huz nae patience, aw the tact o' a sledgehammer 'n' she's stuck in a time warp. She believes in the auld waiys 'n' really toils wi' new stuff, especially the new ideas thit youngsters huv oan fashion."

Jean continued, "That's spot on. Lizzie struggles wi' organising the troops 'n' throws a wobbly at oany new suggestions. Ah dae aw the people stuff 'n' material orders, so Lizzie kin focus on her forte. She's best working oan the kilts plus the fleeces 'n' wee camo puffer jaikets for colder times ay the year. The warriors ur hardy wee beasts but they still like her extra layers in winter. Talking ay warriors, Lizzie disnae half huv a soft spot, fir that Hannibal. She caws him Devil-skin (pronounced Divil Skin) when she sees him or hears that he's got into bother. Aye, Ah guess we'll jist huv tae tolerate her flaws, tae keep her onboard. Jist keep her believin' she's the clothing boss 'n' it'll be grand."

Lulu and The Boss both laughed, knowingly.

Jean then asked Lulu, "Huv oany trainees been strugglin' or hud any issues since we chatted last week?"

"Naw thur aw daein' weel wi' the trainin' 'n' other thin the usual competition amongst the group, they git oan fine. The African Haggi ur really great athletes 'n' tak' info on board really weel, despite some Jockanese difficulties. Ah think they miss family but they're a tight wee group 'n' that helps."

At that, Lulu decided that the training ground beckoned. She stood up, rinsed her cup out, said her goodbyes and off she went.

"Ah reckon Ah'm done here tae, lots tae be gittin' oan wi'… See yiz later," said Lorraine the Sourceror as she, too, took her leave.

The remaining two Haggi women chatted for a few minutes more, then tidied up and made to leave. As they went outside, The Boss asked Jean, "Oh, one last thing, how are things wi' Eddie 'n' kitchen supplies?"

"Ye ken Eddie, jist keeps himsel' tae himsel', sticks tae his routine. He disnae say much, just keeps grafting 'n' daein' a gid job. Plenty fresh fruit 'n' veg fur the kitchen team tae dae oor thing."

*

Meanwhile, out on a secluded part of Huntsmen Hill, Eddie Wood, the octogenarian Haggi gardener, was unaware he was being discussed elsewhere.

Eddie was digging over a section of allotment ground, in readiness for planting. He was a grafter, no doubt about that. Always finding jobs to do and keeping busy.

The tender of the Haggi allotments wore a blue boiler suit, rather than Highland clothing, as was his preference. His thin, grey hair was covered by a green baseball hat with an inscription, in white letters, FF *Champs '48, '51, '52.*

Chapter 21

Back at Auchterbarn Primary, the pupils were on morning break.

Hannibal needed to let Duncan know that the Haggi were around, so he sipped some Haggi Special Water and became invisible. He found Duncan in the playground and tugged his hand, to get him to bend down a bit.

Hannibal whispered, "I need to speak to you. Go to the boys' toilet in two minutes, I'll wait in the first open cubicle."

Duncan said to Davy that he needed to pee and was going to the toilet so his friend didn't wonder why he'd just wandered off.

He walked to the boys' toilet and the first cubicle was free.

"Psst, I'm in the first one," said the invisible Hannibal.

Duncan stepped in and closed the door as Hannibal started to explain that he was at the school with Sparky and Strummer. He added that things were likely to kick off with the bullies, so to be ready to act whenever he called.

Soon after Hannibal started speaking, Gus Burgan had come into the toilet. He headed for the urinal and heard faint talking, coming from one of the cubicles.

"I saw you coming in. You talking to yourself again, Dafty

Dunc? First sign of madness, so they say."

Hannibal put his finger over his lips to indicate to Duncan not to say anything. He gave a quick thumbs-up sign, patted Duncan on the shoulder, then slipped under the cubicle door and exited the toilet area, unseen.

Duncan stayed put in the cubicle for what seemed like an age. To his great relief, eventually Gus banged on his cubicle door but left without saying or doing anything else.

The bell went and everyone went back inside for the pre-lunch lesson. Nothing much happened until the lunch break, then *all hell broke loose*.

Duncan had been separated from Davy in the playground and was out of his sight. An invisible Hannibal climbed up onto Duncan's shoulders to get a message over.

"Davy's in big trouble, the twins huv goat um. Git roond there, right intae thae bullies, gie thum laldy 'n' we'll be in at yir back, tae help ye," shouted Hannibal.

Duncan didn't feel his usual trepidation at all. Fuelled by adrenaline, he sprinted round the corner to go to the aid of his only true pal.

A sizeable crowd of pupils had created a ring and were chanting, "Fight, fight," but Duncan barely saw the bystanders. His focus was on Gus and Eric Burgan, looming over a grounded and terrified Davy.

Years of frustration and hurt were unloaded as Duncan stepped forward and punched an unsuspecting Gus, with a solid right hand. Gus went down but so did Eric... without Duncan even touching him. The wound-up, invisible, tartan-clad warriors had battered right into the bullies, just behind Duncan. They initially got the bullies off balance by pulling at their arms and kicking their ankles and knees, then knocked their legs out from under them with skilled leg sweeps.

It was then time to 'pile in'.

Hannibal helped initially, then largely stood back as Strummer and Sparky, affectionately known within the Haggi world as Search and Destroy, went into a whirlwind of action. Whilst completely unseen by their prey, they rapidly rained well-aimed kicks, punches and elbow strikes into the Burgan bully boys.

Duncan had enjoyed his newfound boldness and landed another few digs at his prior tormentors, while they were down.

Both the bullies were dumbfounded, had no clue what had happened and couldn't believe that this was all Duncan's work. The onslaught continued for another minute or so, until both bullies ended up curled in the foetal position, trying to protect themselves.

By the time a combination of three teachers and Jimmy the Janitor rushed out of the main school building to break up the fight, the big tough bullies were thoroughly defeated. Their clothes were in a right old state and, more importantly, the number of cuts, bumps and bruises they had were quite shocking and testament to a **richt gid kickin'** in Haggi speak.

White faced with shock and surprise, the bullies shielded their embarrassed and battered faces from the bystanders, as they tried to skulk away.

Then things got worse, as Gus started to cry.

His twin, Eric, looked on sheepishly and was unimpressed, to say the least.

As this happened, all the spectating pupils started to cheer and applaud.

A chant of, "Dunc, Dunc, Dunc!" went up and continued

for some time, as the other pupils revelled in the humiliating defeat of Gus and Eric. Duncan was somewhat mortified but also had a feeling of immense pride as a saved and largely uninjured Davy high-fived him and grinned from ear to ear.

That's your reign of terror well and truly over, bully boys, thought the two friends as they looked over at the disappearing, vanquished twin bullies.

As the crowd of pupils started to disperse, Davy was separated from Duncan as other bemused pupils checked that he was OK.

Duncan stayed where he was but noticed faint outlines of bubbles nearby, then heard Hannibal's voice say, "Well done, Duncan, we need tae mak oorsels scarce the noo. Baith ay ye come tae the horseshoe by the burn the night, eftir yir dinner, 'n' Ah'll explain."

None of the other pupils had heard Hannibal speaking but Duncan gave a discreet thumbs-up to show he'd heard and understood his hairy ally.

The new hero of the hour was still euphoric but instinctively knew there was trouble to come and that a visit to the head would be a certainty. He looked around, quickly pulled Davy aside and quietly said, "Davy, there's way more to this than meets the eye, buddy, stuff I've not been able to tell you yet. We're going to get hauled up before Peacock," the head teacher, "so just keep details to a bare minimum and I promise, I'll explain everything after school."

Right on cue, Mr Peacock appeared and summoned the two pals to his office to explain themselves. As they made their way indoors and along the corridor to the head's office, Duncan whispered, "Remember, Davy – play it cool, minimum info."

Chapter 22

As would be expected, the four human fight participants were to be spoken to individually by the head.

Davy was called in first. Duncan was made to wait outside the office, accompanied by a classroom assistant. The erstwhile bullies were having their injuries treated by the school nurse in the medical room.

Parents would no doubt be called in due course but, for now, it was time to get to the bottom of things.

Mr Peacock was a small, skinny man in his fifties. He had pallid colouring, due to a lot of time spent indoors, at school and on his church and bridge club activities. His hair was mostly gone to grey and he wore round, black-framed glasses, perched on his nose.

He was dwarfed by his large desk, looking very serious and addressed Davy. "Well, young Master Smith, we've not seen you in here before, so what's happened today?"

Davy was apprehensive, despite being a victim in the day's events. He was also mindful of Duncan's 'play it cool' prompting.

Davy and Duncan had always had the mentality that you don't grass up other pupils, otherwise things got worse. This was especially so when the people being grassed up, were also the biggest bullies in the school. However, in light of today's events, the reign of the bullies was likely over and he had an opportunity to press home the victim position.

"Well, sir, it was just like a lot of other days where the Burgan twins give myself, Duncan and a load of other kids a hard time, both verbally and physically. They've terrorised us and made our lives a misery for years and until today we've just taken their bullying and given them money, sweets or food to leave us alone."

"That's a big allegation but let's deal with today's altercation for now. Talk me through it please, step by step," replied the head teacher, stonily.

"Well I had had lunch and was alone in the playground. Gus and Eric had threatened, and taken stuff off, other kids, then it was my turn. I was really scared and they're much bigger than me. They said, 'Give us your cash or you're getting a doing.' I said, 'I've not got any money, I just spent it.' They called me a jobbie-faced liar and pushed me over, one of them kicked me. I closed my eyes then, the next thing I saw, Duncan, my best friend, was there and fought off Gus and Eric. That's what happened."

"I see... You're sure of your facts... nothing else to add?" asked Peacock.

"Yes I'm sure, sir, I don't know anything else."

Davy was mightily relieved when the head teacher told him he was free to go.

He got up and left the room.

As he walked out, Davy winked at his bestie and whispered, "Played it cool, minimal info." He then said more loudly, "You've to go in now, Dunc."

The classroom assistant sitting with Duncan didn't hear the first whispered comment.

Duncan got up from his chair and went in. He was asked for his version of events by Mr Peacock.

"Well it was lunchtime and I was inside. Someone shouted that Davy was getting set on by the bullies, so I ran round to help him. Davy was on the ground with Gus and Eric hitting him. I normally don't do anything but I just snapped after years of their bullying and punched Gus Burgan. I then managed to get Gus and Eric away from Davy and that was that. I'm not a fighter but I'm glad I fought back for once and that Davy is OK."

"Mmmm, that sounds all very short and sweet, Duncan. The version of events that I received from the teachers, who intervened, included a lot more than one punch and some restraining. Are you sure there's nothing to add?"

"It all happened so fast, sir, I can't really remember anything else."

Mr Peacock was far from convinced by Duncan's 'evidence' but, in the absence of him saying anything more, had no other option but to let him go. He dismissed Duncan after cautioning him that parents would be informed of the day's events and there may well be repercussions.

After being patched up by the nurse, Gus and Eric Burgan were interviewed separately by Mr Peacock. He had no prior knowledge of the alleged bullying activities of the twin brothers in primary seven. His first impressions of them were that they certainly had the bulk to carry off their alleged bullying activities. In saying that, their meek demeanour and considerable visible injuries, painted a very different picture.

The twins certainly tried to use this to their advantage

during their 'interviews'. They both denied any wrongdoing today, or on any other day, and protested their innocence.

The head teacher did catch them both out with differing, implausible answers to how the teachers, who intervened, had found over forty pound coins plus sundry items of chocolate on the ground around the fight area!

With the interviews of the four fight participants completed, Mr Peacock spent the next hour speaking with teachers, prefects, Jimmy the Janitor and other pupils, taking many of them out of classes to do so.

The common consensus was that:-

1. The Burgan boys were definitely serial bullies, who wreaked havoc on the school population.

2. Duncan was a timid and non-violent boy, who had acted totally out of character.

3. Davy was a vulnerable and easy target, who was in the wrong place at the wrong time.

Mr Peacock was seething that he had been unaware of any of this prior to today's incident. He took to blaming all and sundry for knowing, but not acting, regarding the bullying activity.

Not for one minute, did the head teacher consider that his closed-shop methods and dour, unapproachable personality, were also significant factors.

All four fight participants were kept out of afternoon classes to avoid disruption and to await decisions on any punishments.

Mr Peacock was back in his office, fuming behind the closed door, while his assistant tried to get the respective parents on the phone. The head teacher wanted to brief them on what had happened then decide and communicate any punishments.

The bruised and battered Burgan twins were seated in the library, which was a novelty for them given their disinterest in books or learning tools of any kind. They'd been well warned to keep away from Davy and Duncan or there would be big trouble.

The conversation between the brothers was very limited, as they licked their wounds and started to understand that their reign of invincibility was over.

Eventually Eric said, "You're just a big Jessie, greetin' like a wee lassie."

"Just shut it, you, it really hurt. Didn't see you backing me up much."

Silence returned and they sat staring into space, awaiting their summons for sentencing.

Meanwhile the double D duo opted for a seat in the open air of the school grounds, as it wasn't raining or cold.

Duncan said, "Let's find a seat, Davy, I've got a lot to tell you. This is going to take a while."

Duncan told his friend the complete tale of the crazy sequence of events, starting with the graveyard discussion with Grandad Hamish.

Davy never spoke throughout. He just stared at Duncan, totally enthralled, with the wonder of the tale overcoming his slight annoyance at being kept in the dark till now.

Duncan got to the end and said that the next stage, after school, was meeting the actual Haggi in person and they were BOTH invited.

Davy thought that his admiration for Duncan couldn't go any higher than it already was, but it just had.

They sat in a weird silence for ten minutes beyond the end of Duncan's epic story.

They were summoned inside by the classroom assistant that had sat with them earlier. It was time for the head teacher's verdict.

Mr Peacock ushered them both into his office at the same time.

The head teacher got right to it.

"I don't condone violence in any way but you, Master Smith, are the victim and have nothing to answer for. Master McPherson, you acted aggressively but were acting with historic frustrations and mitigating circumstances, as you were seeking to help your friend. In the circumstances, you will face no punishment on the proviso that your name is not brought to my attention again, any time soon. You are free to go, boys, but don't let me see you in here again."

They left quickly, happy that they were free, in more than one sense.

The Burgan twins had already been advised that they were to be excluded from school for two weeks and would be on probation monitoring for the remainder of the school term. They would be ineligible for any school events, trips or sporting team selection, throughout the remainder of their time at Auchterbarn Primary School. Their parents were not remotely amused at finding out about their sons' bullying activities and had confirmed they would be applying penalties of their own.

Chapter 23

As Duncan arrived home from school, he thought that Cath would make a big deal of the shame of a call to her work from the head teacher. He puffed his cheeks out and opened the door, expecting a hard time.

Since her mum had told Mary the outline of the day's events, Mary had been revelling in not being the one in trouble, for a change. As she heard the front door open, Mary quietly took her place on the stairs and tuned in, expecting things to kick off.

Both siblings were surprised, to say the least, when Cath just stepped forward, hugged Duncan and said, "I don't like fighting, son, but well done for standing up for you and your pal. Sit down and tell me all about it."

Mary felt a wave of frustration that her brother was getting such an easy time, but kept listening.

Duncan retold the story of the bullies fight, which he'd told the head teacher. He added a little more detail and honesty but left out any mention of the Haggi. Duncan then backtracked and told the harrowing tale of how himself and Davy had been bullied for years. He delivered this in a matter-of-fact and emotionless way, which was quite unnerving.

Tears streamed down Cathy's face as she absorbed her son's pain but also her own regrets at only hearing this now, after the event. Even Mary was moved by what she was hearing and she now saw her detached and socially awkward brother in a new light.

Cath eventually said, "Dunc, you need to promise me that in future you tell me about any bad stuff that's going on. I'm not the enemy, I'm your mum. I know I said well done for standing up for Davy and yourself but punching someone is wrong and morally I feel like I should ground you for a couple of days at least."

It was said very calmly but Duncan's reply still surprised her.

He said, "I get it, Mum, and it's your house, your rules, I totally respect that. But for tonight I'm going to have to take my one and only ever opt-out, as I need to make sure Davy is OK and check in with some new friends, TONIGHT."

Cath was quite stunned at Duncan's firmness and resolve. She knew that Davy was his only friend, as far as she was aware.

Maybe his recent altered behaviour is driven by these new friends.

She reluctantly agreed that he could have his 'opt-out' tonight but emphasised that future 'Mum sanctions' would be set in stone.

Mary was astonished and intrigued, in equal measure, now sure that she would shadow Duncan when he left the house later. The elder sibling got up off the stairs and went to her room, still not quite believing what she'd just heard.

After a muted family dinner round the kitchen table, Duncan got up, put his coat on and headed out, as he'd negotiated with Cath earlier. As he got to the front door, he turned and said, "Thanks for your understanding, Mum. I won't be late back."

He opened the front door and stepped out on his way to meet his 'friends'.

Davy was waiting at their usual meet-up point at the end of the street and the two pals hurried, excitedly, towards the burn area. Neither Davy nor Duncan had any inkling that Mary was tailing them on the way to their gathering.

Three Haggi were already in place, as the boys headed for the rendezvous. Sparky was still buzzing from the earlier scrap with the bullies and wasn't sure why he'd been brought along, as Hannibal could easily explain everything himself. Steely had also travelled down with them from Huntsmen Hill for the meeting.

"Why um Ah here, A1?" enquired Sparky.

"Soft skills development, laddie. Yiv goat the fighting skills as displayed at the school but subtle ye ain't. Steely 'n' yirsel ur here fur back up in case thir's oany funny business, nae thit Ah'm expectin' oany bother. Maybe ye kin learn a bit aboot handlin' communication 'n' keepin' folks oan board."

Shortly after, Davy and Duncan walked along the bank of the burn and turned into the horseshoe clearing. Hannibal and Sparky were both there, fully visible.

Duncan didn't react as he had seen Hannibal before but Davy just stood there transfixed and dumbstruck at the wee furry beings standing in front of him.

Hannibal got to it and made the round of introductions.

Davy still didn't move or speak.

Duncan had fully explained earlier about the Haggi but the real-life version was spellbinding.

Hannibal started to speak. "We yased invisibility tae help

ye today 'n' as yir connected noo, Ah reckon ye need tae understand how it works. The story ay how Haggi kin become invisible is a long one, Ah'll try tae keep it as short as possible. Aw the names Ah'm gonnae mention ur Haggi folks thit ye dinnae ken, jist bear wi' me.

"The Clan Wood emblem 'n' motto link thum tae sailing 'n' waves, therefore they huv historic links tae water. Auld Wullie Wood wiz a Haggi diver back in the day 'n' fished the sea 'n' rivers. His sons cairried oan the later part. They wur responsible fir the purification o' the burn water 'n' diverting some o' the purified water through a secret pipe, fir Haggi specific yis. One day, a while back, Elsie Brunton wiz daein' some water trainin' wi' Haggi trainees 'n' some, weirdly, wur wearin' thon sun tan cream. When they pit thur feet intae the purified water, thur taes seemed tae bubble 'n' go blurry. Elsie noticed this 'n' tae cut a very long story short, she telt Handy 'n' Jean Gordon, whit hud happened.

"Between thum, they kept blendin' other ingredients intae the mix until they hud a burn-water-based invisibility potion. This potion only works on Haggi, not humans or other creatures. Oor wee sporrans huv been developed to be Haggi Special Water (HSW) cairriers.

"Handy 'n' Sammy devised a tube/straw mechanism 'n' Lizzie, fae the clothing team, worked oot how tae sew the HSW tube intae the linin' ay Haggi clothing. Ah'll git Sparky tae demonstrate in a mo', bit ye need tae understand thit the invisibility only lasts fir a few minutes; then as it wears off, bubbles appear, then the HSW drinker is revealed. Haggi body parts all go invisible eftir drinkin' HSW 'n' oanythin' they touch'll be invisible tae. That's unless it gets mair thin four feet away fae thir body, then the item becomes visible."

The double D duo couldn't speak as they were too busy trying to take all this in.

"Right, Sparky, tak' a wee sip o' yir HSW 'n' show the laddies how HSW works."

Sparky did as he was asked and two seconds later he was invisible. The boys looked intently around the horseshoe area but saw and heard nothing. Sparky walked about for a few seconds then extended his right arm and tapped Duncan on the shoulder.

Duncan shrieked, farted, and almost jumped out of his skin. Davy jumped too.

"Sorry, guys, couldnae resist," chuckled Sparky.

"Subtle as usual… Mair trainin' required," groaned Hannibal.

As Sparky had only taken a small sip of HSW, within thirty seconds he started to 'bubble'. His outline loosely appeared in bubble form then became clearer and more defined, until he was fully visible again.

"So that's how HSW works, boys," said Hannibal, stating the obvious.

Blocked out behind the bushes, and unseen by the others, Mary had heard, but not seen, the whole conversation and demonstration. She turned to make a run for home to avoid being discovered but instead almost tripped over Steely, who was standing about a yard away from her.

"Whey ur you?" asked Steely.

"I'm Mary, Duncan's big sister. Who or what the hell are you, more like?" angrily retorted a shocked Mary.

Steely recognised both the danger posed by the intruder and her possible importance and stature, assuming that she was who she said she was.

"Move… wur goin' tae yer brother," instructed Steely in a

determined voice.

Mary's legs were like jelly but she complied and started to walk, being guided, from behind, by Steely.

As Steely marched Mary along the bank of the burn and into the horseshoe den, she stared wide-eyed at the additional two Haggi warriors in front of her.

"Oh, wow... I CAN'T WAIT to tell Mum and the girls about this... freak show," said Mary, smugly.

Duncan scowled at his sister in absolute horror and despair. *There's no way she can be allowed to wreck this.*

Steely explained that Mary had been lurking nearby, was supposedly Duncan's sister, and had heard their discussion.

Duncan confirmed, "She is my sister and nosey with it." He sighed deeply then continued, "Mary, for once, can you just keep a lid on something? This is way more important than you can imagine."

"What... three hairy, tartan puppets that can talk and walk without human input? No way can this stay secret," she replied.

Hannibal stayed quiet but started to extend his legs, to make himself taller.

He doubled his height then stopped, lowered his legs back into their normal position, moved slightly towards Mary, came to a halt about a yard from her and extended his arm all the way across to her, as if to shake hands.

Mary was visibly shocked at his ability. She backed away from Hannibal, almost falling over.

Hannibal extended his arm, still further, then put his hand into Mary's. He shook her hand gently but with a firm grip. He then started to talk in his best proper English, and said, "Haggi Warrior Hannibal Bisset, at your service. Pleased to meet you."

His politeness and change in speech, from what she'd heard earlier, caught Mary completely off guard. Hannibal retracted his arm then started to speak, softly. "Mary, you are young and impetuous like many your age, but Duncan is right in what he said. Your Grandad Hamish has a long connection with us Haggi and he is revered by our kind. His family have been promised Haggi protection, in lieu of our debt to him in saving our environment and way of life. As Hamish's blood, you will have access to that protection and help. Your brother was struggling and asked for our help. You can see that we're helping him already. You, yourself, will need our help too.

You maybe don't think so right now. It might be next week, next month, a year from now, who knows… but YOU WILL NEED OUR HELP AT SOME POINT. I *implore* you to keep the Haggi existence and location under complete secrecy. If you tell ANYONE, can you live with what it will do to your brother and his relationship with you? Would you so easily destroy hundreds of years of history, a way of life and a whole colony in your community? Are you willing to trash your grandfather's legacy, leave yourself unprotected and remove your own source of readily accessible help?"

Mary was visibly wavering from her initial position, as Hannibal's words registered with her. She still had an element of defiance in her voice as she said, "OK, I'll maintain my silence, for now. But… if you fail me or let me down, I'll tell the world."

She noticeably lost her spark, her shoulders sagging a little, as she agreed to maintain the Haggi secret.

"Good. Thank you, Mary. We'll have your back, I promise," said Hannibal.

Duncan exhaled a breath of relief that they had persuaded his belligerent sister into silence, at least for now.

Davy, who had listened intently throughout without really being acknowledged, didn't have any intention of telling ANYONE about tonight's events, he was just satisfied being part of it all and close to Duncan.

The three humans made their way home without another word being said, the trio now bonded in knowledge and silence.

As the three kids left the scene, Sparky realised that Hannibal had handled things impeccably through courtesy, reasoning and softening behaviour and language.

So that's what soft skills are all about.

Hannibal beckoned his two colleagues to head back to HHHQ and said a silent prayer that his plea for Mary's silence had been truly successful.

Later, Duncan lay awake in his bed. It was near the end of the most amazing day ever but sleep wouldn't come. He replayed the day's events many times, knowing that Davy could be trusted implicitly and hoped against hope, that Mary would keep her word and her silence.

Chapter 24

After the bully fight incident at the primary school, a speedy update report had been made to Haggi HQ by Sparky.

The update included two things.

Firstly, an 'in-the-field' decision had been made and the school bullies had been tackled by Duncan McPherson with Haggi backing. All had gone well with no issues – no immediate further action was required.

Secondly, Duncan's information, regarding his teacher's drink problem, was deadly accurate. It was a slam dunk, so the Senior Council had quickly authorised a *'put a scare on'*. Haggi warriors, Strummer and Lulu, were to be dispatched to Rowena Robinson's rural cottage to deliver a 'wake up' message, that night.

Strummer and Lulu were often paired together on missions, as they were very good at what they did and had a shared passion for music.

*

From Rowena's perspective, Monday had been a bit of a blur.

She had managed to visit several of her drink stashes at

school and partaken of wine throughout the day. She vaguely remembered hearing something about a big pupil fight and that two of her pupils were absent after lunch. This last bit was a bit sketchy but she thought it might have been the two quiet pals that had missed the afternoon lesson.

Not sure though.

Rowena had managed to drive home without hitting anyone or anything with her car. This was a very fortunate result, given she was well over the drink-driving limit.

On getting home, she had no thought of food, only her beloved drink.

She changed out of her work clothes and straight into her PJs and dressing gown. A bottle of red wine was cracked open and Rowena sat eagerly back in her chair, glass in hand.

The six o'clock news hadn't yet started.

By half past ten, things had got messy as Rowena was on red wine bottle number three and definitely the worse for wear. She was slumped in a weird position on her armchair and was going, intermittently, in and out of sleep.

Despite shaky hands and blurred vision, she had not spilled a single drop of wine.

The Haggi duo of Strummer and Lulu pulled up outside Rowena's cottage on their Hagg-mobiles in 'sleekit mode' so they hadn't been heard on the way. Due to their liking for music, they'd decided to bring a Haggi-sized guitar on the mission.

As they stealthily entered through the unlocked front door, they couldn't hear anything. Once they made it to the entrance to the kitchen, they started to understand why Duncan had concerns. They spotted the two empty wine bottles plus another almost empty one, sitting on the worktop.

"Really – it's nae even the weekend," said Lulu, not trying to disguise her disapproval.

They subsequently checked the living room and found Rowena slumped in her chair, glass of red, in hand.

"How dae ye fancy playin' this one?" Lulu asked Strummer.

"Well – we huv a guitar, let's play."

Strummer got his guitar strap in place over his shoulder and started to play, ironically, Red Red Wine.

"Red Red Wine… Stay Close To Me…"

As they sang the 'stay close to me' line, Rowena pulled her glass to her and cuddled it.

"Could'nae make that up," said Strummer.

"Tragic," replied his Haggi partner.

Rowena then seemed to stir a bit and become more alert. By this time, the visitors had drunk some Haggi Special Water and become invisible.

They had looped a rope over the centre of the living room curtain pole and attached it to the modern, metal light bracket, near the room centre. The guitar strap was hooked over the taut rope.

As Rowena's eyes opened a bit, all she could see was a mini guitar, floating backwards and forwards across her living room. The Haggi were using their extended arms and taking it in turns to 'zipline' the guitar back and forth to each other.

"How… howsat poss…bile…?" the drunken teacher mumbled.

The guitar stopped in mid-air as the Haggi got fed up with this wee game and turned up the heat.

The duo then got the guitar free, Lulu started playing and they sang adapted lyrics to the tune of Fulsom Prison Blues by Johnny Cash.

The Haggi are a comin'
Wuv come fae up the Hill.
Yer seein' a pink elephant,
We think that ye ur ill.
Ur', stuck in drunken prison
Or poppin' drugs, 'n' high.
Whatever yin's, yer poison
We think, Ur' gonna die.

Rowena was now shaking, sweating buckets and starting to come to her senses even more. Then both Haggi started to 'bubble' as the Special Haggi Water began to wear off.

Lulu took another swig and went invisible again but Strummer continued to become clearer, until he was fully visible to Rowena.

"Wha… Whaaat the heeelll are you?" was all she could get out, then screamed at the top of her lungs.

Strummer didn't elaborate, he just delivered his 'sermon', saying in a determined voice, "Listen up, Ribena… Yeh… news alert… that's what the kids caw ye'. Wur no' here tae play, wur here tae slay… yir drinkin', that is. We ken yiv had a rough gig o'er the last few years but wur providin' the short sharp shock, tae try tae break the cycle. Ye need tae git yirsel sorted 'n' open yer eyes, primarily tae yir ain issues. Nae jist that, but fir young McPherson in yer class. He's no daft, he's mega bright and some drawer, by the way. The laddie needs stretched, nae ignored."

By this point, Rowena was taking a bit more on board but she relapsed, quickly.

Lulu had 'bubbled' and now came into full view. Rowena was fixated on the hugely unusual, copper-coloured eye staring her down. It was accompanied by a normal dark brown eye but the copper one was freaking her out.

Lulu threw in her contribution and said, "We reckin' ye should be layin' off the grape juice 'n' start daein' yirsel some favours. Yiv goat the skills 'n' the passion fur the teachin', thuv jist goat buried under yer grief. Remember we're no' pink elephants, we're fur real. Wu'll be watchin' ye... real close, Ribena... Ye kin coont oan it."

Lulu pointed at her copper-coloured eyeball and gave Rowena the 'watchin' ye' motion with her fingers.

Rowena whimpered softly, determined that she'd never meet these characters or anything like them – EVER AGAIN.

Ms Robinson's musical visitors then left the premises, fairly sure that their scare mission had been successfully carried out. They got on their Hagg-mobiles, adopted 'sleekit mode' and headed for HHHQ.

Rowena was left, sitting on the living room floor, hugging herself and rambling all sorts of gibberish.

"UB40... wee furry creatures... copper eye... stop drinking... Red Red Wine... tartan... Duncan in my class... floating guitar... copper eye... never again... the Haggi are a-coming."

Her rambling continued on a similar vein for another ten minutes, then Rowena Robinson zonked out.

The drink had won, for now.

Chapter 25

On the morning after his bully-bashing activities and Haggi debrief by the burn, Duncan had woken earlier than usual. So much earlier that he easily beat his sister to the breakfast table. He was hugely energised from stepping out of his own fears and Cath noticed that he walked noticeably taller as he made his way into the kitchen.

"How's Auchterbarn's champion boxer this morning?" asked Cath.

"Good thanks, Mum. Things are going to get better from now on… with no more opt-outs."

Cath smiled at her son's newfound optimism and inner resolve.

Mary had eventually surfaced.

Breakfast and getting ready for school played out much as it did every other day. The one major difference, was Duncan inwardly dreading his sister blurting out Haggi information.

Mary was subdued at breakfast, just as she'd been most of Monday at school. The Glam Gang had not mentioned Brad again, staying true to their pledge to 'button it' on that front. The only deviation from this had been a 'What to wear for the Brad date on Friday?' debate between Steph and Mary, when the others weren't around.

Mary had initially been mega impressed that her awkward, shy and timid brother demolished two sizeable, older bullies on his own. After last night's events, she now knew that he'd had considerable 'hairy help' but was sworn to her uneasy secrecy. She had so many more questions for her brother but even she knew that she'd have to chill on it for a while, rather than pushing Duncan for more detail.

As the kids left for school, Cath got her keys ready for locking up and driving to work. They left on their separate paths and Duncan definitely walked with more purpose as he made for his meeting point with Davy.

Davy was already there, gazing admiringly at his hero best pal, as Duncan walked up.

"That was quite something yesterday, Dunc. We won't forget that in a hurry," said a buoyant Davy.

"Too right but we need to keep our chat on this low key. We can't get caught out," Duncan replied.

"That's fine by me. I still can't believe what I saw and heard last night," responded Davy.

They walked on towards school and as they reached the entry gates Jenny Paterson was walking towards them. Duncan's heart rate went through the roof and his mouth, completely dry as she said, "Well done for sorting out those two toerags, Dunc. They had it coming."

As she turned away Jenny accidentally brushed Duncan's arm, setting his senses on fire.

Wow, the most beautiful girl in school touched me and knows my name.

Davy stood, cringing, as his pal gazed longingly after Jenny, while she walked back towards her pals.

In the playground before the first bell, Duncan received various admiring glances, eye contact and thumbs-up from other pupils. There were also noticeable whisperings of his deeds of yesterday being shared amongst groups of newly respectful pupils.

The Burgan bullies didn't appear and were nowhere to be seen for the rest of the school day.

Chapter 26

On the Tuesday morning, Hannibal and Strummer were in position at the primary school.

All was quiet.

Strummer was just finishing updating Hannibal with all the gory details of the Monday-night musical 'scare' at Rowena's cottage. They were primarily here to see if the night-time visit to Ms Robinson had had the desired effect.

"Wait up, looks like it's hud an impact," said Hannibal as Ms Robinson's white Vauxhall Corsa pulled into the staff car park. The time was seven-twenty-eight a.m., more than an hour before she usually showed up.

Rowena got out and locked up her car, moving quickly but nervously, with her head spinning round, like an owl looking for danger. To the trained eyes of the Haggi watchers, 'Ribena' definitely looked 'shook up'. Her hair was a bit dishevelled and jammed into a bobble; her face very pale, no make-up; and the bags under her eyes indicated a sleepless night or nights.

Wonder why that was.

Rowena knew that Jimmy the Janitor unlocked the main entry door, bang on seven-thirty. She checked the surrounding area and, not seeing any sign of the janitor, tried the door handle.

It opened.

Timed it perfectly.

After last night's events, Rowena Robinson, neé Preston, was at school early, to make a start in confronting her drinking demons.

These hidden wine bottles are going… for good.

She decided to go to the staff room first, so made for the top floor, where it was located. There were no other humans around as she moved swiftly up the stairs, a woman on a mission.

She opened the staff room door to find it empty, as she had hoped. Rowena had three secret 'stash' sites in here, where she had hidden smaller bottles, rather than the full-blown ones. In less than a minute, she had retrieved all three mini wine bottles and set off for the girls' toilet on the top floor.

As she opened the toilet door it was, again, free of human activity. Ms Robinson walked quickly to one of the open cubicles, paused briefly, then turned the screw-top lids and poured the contents of all three bottles into the toilet bowl.

She felt nothing much as the toilet flush kicked in and the frothy red liquid disappeared out of sight.

The now empty bottles were tossed into the waste bin.

My classroom next.

Rowena set off down the stairs and was close to reaching her own classroom, when she heard footsteps. Jimmy the Janitor came round the corner and was a bit startled to see Rowena standing right in front of him, as he didn't think anyone was around.

"Morning, hen. You're early this morning, everything OK?" said Jimmy.

Rowena really didn't want to waste any time so politely replied, "Never better but I've got a lot to do before the kids come in."

She hoped this would do the trick and started walking away to avoid getting bogged down in a chat. Jimmy didn't say anything but was intrigued why Ms Robinson was in at this time, as she never usually surfaced till about quarter to nine.

Rowena hurried on to her own classroom and removed the wine bottles from her desk area plus some of the cupboards and drawers in the classroom. Seven bottles in total – five small ones and two full-blown.

She felt a flush of embarrassment when she saw the full extent of her classroom 'stash'. It took two trips to the nearest toilet to dispose of the red liquid but she flushed it all away and disposed of the bottles, without much regret. She then tried to remember where else she had secret tipple hiding places.

The sports hall, gym equipment cupboard was one such site. Ironically, unbeknown to Ms Robinson, Duncan had often used this place as a sanctuary from the twin bullies, Gus and Eric. She checked in the dark, back corner, behind a cluster of gym mats and sure enough, there was a three-quarters-full bottle of red... sitting there, as if taunting her.

Rowena bent forward to pick up the bottle but wavered... and stopped.

Just one won't hurt.

She knew in her heart that it was wrong but turned and walked out of the gym equipment cupboard, then the sports hall. The bottle remained behind.

Rowena walked towards Jimmy the Janitor's domain, a cluttered square room just off the main corridor. Jimmy was known to take a wee drink and Rowena had often shared an illicit swig or two with him, as she used the Janitor's room as another hiding place for her supplies. Having seen him earlier, she decided she couldn't face Jimmy again so soon, so swerved away from his room and vowed to return later and remove the offending bottle.

From there, Ms Robinson went back to her own classroom and tidied up her desk area. She placed the daily registration list on her desk, left a pen sitting beside it and made a return to the staff room.

Harry Houston, one of the primary five teachers, was taking his coat off and putting it on a hanger when Rowena marched into the room.

"Good grief, I nearly ended myself there," said Harry in shock. "I'm usually in twenty minutes before the next person and I've never seen you this early. What's going on?" he continued.

"Couldn't sleep so thought I'd make an early start," replied Ms Robinson, defensively.

The two made small talk for a while and other teachers started arriving. There were quite a few raised eyebrows at seeing Rowena so early and one or two teachers even considered (wrongly) that there was maybe a new thing going between Houston and Robinson.

Eventually, to Rowena's great relief, the staff room started to empty as the various teachers headed off to prepare for the arrival of their charges. She was in place in her own classroom ten minutes before the bell rang to signify the start of another school day. A very unusual occurrence for Ms Robinson.

The classroom was almost full when Davy and Duncan walked in and took their places. The other pupils started to applaud and whoop on the back of the previous day's events and excitedly shared stories of what had happened. Ms Robinson listened initially then shushed the class to quieten them. She then spoke. "I don't particularly condone violence, Duncan, but you did a good thing with your actions against the bullies yesterday. Well done, but remember the pen can be mightier than the sword."

A classroom of confused faces stared at Ms Robinson and this was only enhanced when she, enthusiastically, started the registration roll call. Normally she was dour and offhand till at least ten o'clock but this was a different teacher in class today.

This behavioural revelation continued through the morning, with Ms Robinson really investing time in her pupils and seeking questions rather than a stony silence. At morning break, the whole class had chatted about nothing else than the change in their teacher and yesterday's battering of the bullies.

The later morning teaching continued in a positive vein but was broken by the lunchtime bell. Rowena went out to buy a cheese sandwich at the local corner shop. She ate it and drank a mug of coffee, in the staff room.

She exchanged pleasantries with some fellow teachers but her mind was on the remaining rogue wine bottles.

Ms Robinson knew from his routine that Jimmy the Janitor was never in his wee room in the second half of lunch break, therefore she had a window of opportunity. Having checked the coast was clear, Rowena made her way to the area and moved stealthily into the Janitor's space.

She located her wine bottle but it had a yellow Post-it note attached. It was a message from, she suspected, her Monday night visitors. *Yer havin' a giraffe. Must try harder.*

After dusting herself down, she made her way to the gym

equipment cupboard. Again, Ms Robinson found her bottle, with another Post-it note attached. This time, it said: *Wir incognito, not blind. It's aw' or nothing – dae it for Robbie's memory... if no fir yirsel.*

Chapter 27

Hannibal and Strummer had left the primary school before lunchtime. They we're partially encouraged by what they'd seen from Ms Robinson throughout the morning. Worries remained though, regarding the remaining rogue wine bottles, which Rowena seemed to think didn't count and wouldn't be discovered.

The two Haggi needed some sustenance so decided to go to the town supermarket and work out a plan of action to get fed. They wouldn't outright shoplift their items, as that went against Haggi morals, but they couldn't very well walk in, buy their items and casually walk back out again. They would be compromised and there would be absolute hysteria amongst shoppers and staff alike.

How often do two hairy, two-foot-high, tartan-clad creatures go shopping in a supermarket!

They also didn't carry any cash and had no credit cards available.

By a stroke of luck they found a semi-crisp ten-pound note blowing across the car park as they hugged the line of bushes along the side of the supermarket.

The intrepid Haggi shoppers took sizeable drinks of Haggi

Special Water through their straw mechanisms and became invisible, as they went in through the supermarket entrance. Due to their ten-pound note windfall, they now had the means to buy their lunch.

As they walked to the sandwich section, invisible to staff and shoppers, the Haggi colleagues debated and agreed on their tasty choice. They did a quick scan of the surrounding area and noticed that there were a lot of shoppers in and around their aisle plus, crucially, a member of staff stocking the shelves nearby. In addition, their chosen sandwich pack was high up so they couldn't risk reaching up, as their extended arms would be too far from their bodies and their lunch would be moving and visible. They also couldn't climb up and throw the sandwiches down as this would be highly visible and noisy, so would likely be noticed by the humans.

Therefore, they hatched a plan, cunningly waiting in an invisible state on opposite shelves until a woman with a heavily laden trolley came past. When the female shopper reached out to pick up a filled roll, Strummer made a noise to distract the woman and Hannibal flipped their chosen sandwich pack into her trolley.

The sandwiches landed with barely a sound and no one noticed a thing as the two Haggi made their way back to the floor, giving each other the thumbs-up.

The hungry Haggi had to wait a bit for the shopper to pick up her final few purchases and were starting to worry that their invisibility would wear off. Thankfully, their fears went unfounded and they were still invisible as the lady turned her trolley towards the checkout area.

The trolley pusher was rooting in her purse, seeking out various cards for the checkout while completely unaware that she had two furry passengers on her trolley. As she started unloading her items onto the conveyor belt, Strummer waited till the woman wasn't looking and used his extended arm to flick their sandwiches out of the trolley. When the sandwich pack had fallen almost to the ground, Hannibal deftly 'controlled' it on his right instep and flicked the sandwiches up into his hands, without anyone noticing.

Still got the old fitbaw skills.

From there, the Haggi managed to manoeuvre the sandwiches to the self-serve checkout, without getting rumbled. There were no customers in this area but a section supervisor was wandering around nearby, checking the equipment and tidying baskets away.

"Diversion required, bud," said Hannibal to Strummer, quietly.

Hannibal waved the sandwich pack barcode over the self-service scanner and it beeped, registering the purchase. The supervisor looked round in surprise at the noise, considering how there had been a beep with no one there. At the same instant that the supervisor's suspicion rose, Strummer started running around like an Olympic sprinter. He used his Haggoo barcode on his extended arm to create a crescendo of beeps on multiple scanners, one after the other.

There was 'beeping carnage', like peak time in an amusement arcade, as the demented store supervisor sought to make sense of what was happening. The supervisor was more than distracted for the next two minutes, trying to reset the scanners and restore calm.

In the meantime Hannibal had selected cash payment method, put his ten-pound note through the slot, grabbed his change and regrasped the sandwich pack in his extended hand. He then exited the self-service section in a blur, his wee hairy legs going nineteen to the dozen. His sole focus was on getting to the exit, unseen, and as quickly as possible.

As he sprinted towards the exit doors, he was so distracted that he didn't see the CAUTION – WET FLOOR warning sign, until it was way too late.

His fast-moving Hagg-boots made contact with the spilled orange juice from a leaky carton, and his feet went from under him.

He started to fall backwards but his feet accelerated on towards the exit.

Their precious pack of sandwiches was catapulted through the air, up and over a special offers display, and was fully visible to all the humans in the area.

Strummer was also running fast but was nearer the exit. He turned to look back as Hannibal did his inadvertent flying, horizontal manoeuvre.

Trying hard to stifle his laughter, Strummer seamlessly adjusted his stride and caught their airborne lunch, which became invisible again, as soon as he caught it. Hannibal was also invisible but it was impossible not to hear the thud and his loud groan of pain as he crashed into the special offers display.

The security guard at the door certainly heard the thump and Hannibal's deep groan. He also could have sworn that he had just seen a pack of sandwiches flying at close to warp speed, then just disappearing.

The guard was distracted by a clothes tag alarm going off and didn't have time to intervene before the Haggi were out the door.

Both Haggi started to 'bubble' with their invisibility wearing off, so ran round to a quiet corner of the car park and went into the bushes to avoid detection.

"Wow, Ah didnae ken ye wir plannin' oan a fresh orange accompaniment fur oor sannies," sniggered Strummer.

"Shut yir hole, Ah could've been knocked unconscious wi' ma heid skelpin' the flair," retorted a shaken Hannibal.

"Nae chance ay a brain injury, that's fur shair. Plus wi' aw that hair ay yours, yer heid wid be cushioned like a pillae," added Strummer.

"Mightae kent there'd be nae sympathy fur ma wee accident," grumped A1.

"You'd be knottin' yirsel if it wiz me thit goat banjoed," responded Strummer.

"It wiz a belter, right enough," said Hannibal and the two of them went into fits of laughter as they replayed the tale of the Haggi flying sannies.

They eventually calmed down and ate their sannies on their journey back to the primary school.

The hairy duo returned not long into the post-lunch afternoon session. They were just in time to see Ms Robinson walk out into the school grounds and take a seat on a bench in the distance. She had left the class with a task and made an excuse to go outside.

Just need a few minutes to clear my head.

Rowena sat on the bench staring straight ahead, deep in thought.

She jolted in surprise, as Jocky Pearson, a fellow teacher, sat down beside her.

"Hi... wondered why you're out here at this time... Penny for your thoughts," said Jocky, with a half-smile. He sat back, wrung his hands, then fidgeted with his shirt collar.

Rowena amazed herself with the honesty of her reply

when she said, "I'm having a tough time and need a friend, who isn't in a bottle. I have a drink problem and today, I'm trying to stop."

"Wow. That's heavy-duty stuff, Rowena... but you're very much not alone. Believe it or not, I was pretty much in your shoes about a month ago... but... my mate... got me to go... to a meeting... an AA meeting. I haven't touched a drop since," said Jocky.

Their short conversation continued and led to an agreement that Rowena would be attending an Alcoholics Anonymous meeting with her fellow teacher – SOON.

The Haggi were too far away to hear the exchange between the teachers. They did, however, have a good feeling about it, as the teachers went back into the school to resume their teaching activities.

The afternoon session rolled on and the final school bell of the day indicated home time. As her pupils left for the day, Ms Robinson felt emboldened with new energy and optimism.

I've got a great idea and I'm going to the head with it, right now.

She tidied up, picked up her bag and less than five minutes later, Rowena knocked on the door of her head teacher. She identified herself and was beckoned in by Mr Peacock, who had had a busy couple of days in the aftermath of the bullies incident.

"Afternoon, Ms Robinson. Don't see you here often, what can I do for you?" asked Mr Peacock.

"I wish to put forward a suggestion to benefit the pupils, especially the more... vulnerable ones."

"Sounds interesting. What do you have in mind?"

"Bear with me, while I expand on my idea. The basic suggestion is installing a bright yellow '*Sunshine Seat*', where pupils could go and sit if they feel sad, threatened, lonely… whatever. The idea would be that others, seeing a fellow pupil in need, would join them on the Sunshine Seat and try to help them. Bring brightness into lives, could even be the slogan."

She was thinking out loud now, and on a roll. Rowena continued, "If the school covers what the purpose of the Sunshine Seat is in advance, say through newsletters and an announcement in assembly, then pupils and parents will know what it's about. The seat shouldn't be too central or obvious but should be visible from the staff room. No Big Brother CCTV but teachers and prefects could monitor goings on around the Sunshine Seat and therefore provide insight and an advance warning system of issues. A rota maybe? That's about it."

The head teacher leaned back and said, "Interesting," as he thought back to yesterday and how he had been unaware of the bullying issues. Then his cynical side kicked in and he continued, "I can see some merit in this, Ms Robinson, but let's not kid ourselves. Regrettably, in the real world, unpopular, different, sad or lonely kids don't just suddenly get instant help or are magically accepted. I could see this becoming a source of ridicule and even making things worse."

"Well it might be idealistic but surely if they gain one friend or ally, they're better off than their start point," Rowena responded, with her own recent bench encounter very much to the forefront of her mind. She continued, "What's the saying? For evil to triumph, all it takes is for good men to do nothing. Something like that. Surely, as the custodians of our pupils from Monday to Friday, we should try to develop better awareness of possible issues and protect their wellbeing. That way we can prevent and help, rather than shutting ourselves off and abandoning the kids to their fate."

Mr Peacock was impressed with Rowena's robust defence of her idea as he replied, "Good points, well made. How about you leave this with me, I'll take some soundings, and we'll see from there?"

Rowena had a horrible feeling that she was being fobbed off but politely said, "That sounds good, thank you for your time."

She turned, walked out of the head teacher's office and jauntily made her to her car.

The once again invisible Haggi duo followed Ms Robinson out of Mr Peacock's office and watched her get in her car to drive home. She seemed like a new person and they really hoped their Post-it notes had had some impact.

As Jimmy the Janitor made his rounds before lock-up, Hannibal and Strummer went into his room to check the bottle situation.

Rowena's wine bottle that was there earlier, was GONE.

They then made their way to the gym equipment cupboard for their secondary check.

There WAS a wine bottle there but *it had no alcohol in it.*

A hand-written reply note from Rowena Robinson was folded inside the bottle.

I'm fully on board, whoever or whatever you are.
NO MORE DRINK!!!
PS I'm doing this for ME and my PUPILS.

"Progress, indeed," said Strummer, as he gave a thumbs-up and started to whistle Always Look on the Bright Side of Life.

Hannibal, nodded, chuckled, and the two Haggi colleagues left the school, heading for Huntsmen Hill.

Chapter 28

At their first meeting, Duncan had flagged concern to Hannibal about his sister Mary's potential involvement with a much older boy at her school. Hannibal also had sizeable concerns and had shared his thoughts, in his debrief to the power brokers.

The Haggi Senior Council had considered the situation and authorised Haggi surveillance on this older boy. Through years of experience, they recognised that, generally, girls matured much quicker than boys through their teens, and often beyond. Even so, they would not allow Hamish McPherson's granddaughter to come to any harm. While she was a beautiful, well-developed girl with hormones in overdrive, Mary would not be thirteen for another fortnight.

Best buddies, Sammy the Tammie and Punnet, were tasked with related shadowing and information gathering. They knew, via Duncan, that Brad Thomas was supposed to take Mary on their first 'date' on the coming weekend. The Haggi pals decided they'd check Brad out in the days leading up to his liaison with Mary.

Their findings were alarming.

Brad wasn't far short of his seventeenth birthday and lived

in a one-parent household, with his alcoholic mother. His hippy, pot-smoking and free-loving biological father had long since moved on to pastures new. Illegal substances and loose rules were, therefore, ingrained in Brad's DNA.

From what the Haggi had uncovered, Brad seemed to be a magnet to schoolgirls. The female school grapevine had him badged as the coolest, best-looking guy around. His tattoos and likeness to a few current music stars gave him the bad-boy rep that sucked girls in.

Related Haggi surveillance notes
Monday evening/night
- Brad was in Grange Park most of the night.
- He was in the company of a younger girl from his school.
- Alcohol and illegal smoking substances were part of proceedings.
- The young girl was noticeably uncomfortable with Brad's intentions towards her.

Tuesday evening/night
- Brad didn't drink any alcohol or meet anyone.
- He stayed at home, in his room, but couldn't remember much, as he was heavily stoned.
- Brad didn't make it to school in the morning.

Wednesday night
- See Monday but with a different girl.

By this point, Duncan and Hannibal's initial warnings were flashing bright red with danger.

The Haggi pals had seen enough.

The teenage heartthrob was now a marked man and a clear plan was put in place to save Mary from both herself, and Brad Thomas.

Mary was scheduled to meet Brad at seven-thirty p.m. on Friday at the entrance to Grange Park, on the east side of Auchterbarn. The two Haggi located young Brad at seven p.m. He was already inside Grange Park, sitting on a bench near the line of trees, which followed the route of the burn.

Brad had already drunk a sizeable amount of straight vodka but had plenty more in his pockets for 'later.' He was smoking a chunky spliff of illegal substances and was considerably 'mellowed'.

The Haggi had consumed Haggi Special Water, so were invisible and could move around freely, without detection. They had got close to Brad without him having any idea they were there and otherwise, the park was deserted.

"How's it goin', Brad ma boy?" Sammy asked, from the shadows.

Brad's head lifted slowly, wondering who was speaking. His glazed eyes surveyed the area around the bench he was sitting on. He saw nothing and took another slow drag on his spliff.

"Dae ye ayeways need vodka, tae get the lassies tae like ye?" said Sammy, in follow-up.

"No, they love me, man," Brad replied to the invisible presence.

"Ah heard that ye often say, yil try oanything once, is that right?" challenged Punnet.

"That's my motto, bring it on."

A bottle of reddish-coloured Haggi Berry Brew floated towards the Casanova Bad Boy.

"Try this then," Punnet suggested, walking slowly towards Brad, with the bottle in the hand of his fully extended right arm.

Brad was extremely confused at this drink, floating freely in mid-air.

Maybe I've had more than I thought.

However, general intrigue and his reputation ensured that he would, inevitably, drink the mysterious liquid. Brad duly obliged, drinking the full bottle in less than a minute.

Drinking that amount of Berry Brew can knock out a bull elephant, so Brad Thomas had no chance. He was soon sound asleep, with limbs like rubber bands.

The Haggi had brought a Hagg-mobile and trailer with them to transport Brad away from the park. The teenage heartthrob was a well-built lad and Sammy and Punnet took several attempts to heave him onto the trailer.

Punnet checked the park, saw no one, selected 'sleekit mode' and drove away, noiselessly, towards the Thomas house. A harsh lesson was being delivered but they wanted to ensure that young Brad was returned home safely.

Punnet drove Sleeping Beauty back home on the Hagg-mobile, taking things steadily so as not to tip his human cargo onto the road. As Punnet pulled up at the Thomas residence, a couple of other Haggi stepped out from around the side of the house. They were well-built lads, ideal for the task at hand, with particularly impressive beards and wearing appropriate clan tartan kilts with accompanying red beanie hats. These Haggi were brothers, called Frazer (known as Fraz) and Ronnie and hailed from the Aberdeen branch of Clan Fraser.

"Fit like Punnet, did awthin' goan tae plan?" asked Ronnie.

"Aye, nae probs, let's get Bradley Boy tae his scratcher,"

retorted Punnet.

Between the three of them, they bundled Brad off the Haggmobile trailer. Then, having extracted Brad's house key from his pocket, they opened the door, half carried, half dragged him up the front steps, and bundled him into his house.

Brad's mum was fast asleep in a drunken stupor, so never heard or saw a thing.

Once they had Brad in his own room, they took off his coat and shoes.

"Stick ahm flat on his back the noo," instructed Punnet.

"Wid eh nae be bitter oan eh's side, so eh disnae puke 'n' choke?" cautioned Fraz.

"This'll only tak a sec, thin he can go intae recovery position," replied Punnet, with a devilish expression on his face.

The Fraser brothers shrugged and stood back, just as Punnet jumped up on the bed and booted young Brad, hard, flush in the sore bits.

"That's for Mary, ya wee scrote."

Punnet had made one minor error though. He'd made the kick with his shorter leg.

On the follow through from the blow, he lost his balance on the wobbly bed, almost toppling over.

This just increased his ire at Brad, so Punnet rebalanced, swapped legs and booted him in the plums again, saying, "An' that's fir aw the other lassies, bawbag."

Fraz and Ronnie looked at each other, making a mental note. *Dinnae mess wi' Punnet.* But they didn't intervene or say anything.

The three Haggi then quietly rolled a still-comatose Brad into the appropriate safe position on his side. They didn't linger, turned and left Brad to sleep off his excesses. It would take a while!

On the basis of their recent surveillance, Sammy had stayed in the park and was joined by Handy. They had done a check of the best locations and had quickly set up several tiny cameras and microphones. The surveillance equipment was provided courtesy of big Tony (Haggi E2), the Hagg technical wizard. Sammy was pretty sure that dodgy Brad wasn't going to change his ways and they needed evidence of his actions.

The equipment had been up and running for a few minutes, when a nervous but excited Mary came into view. It was bang on seven-thirty.

In preparation for her date, Mary had skilfully applied full make-up before she left number twenty-eight. Her hair was down and had been straightened. She wore a simple, light blue top under a denim jacket. A well-fitting, but not too tight, pair of jeans and white pumps completed her outfit.

A first impression of her, based on appearance, would have placed her age at fifteen, maybe sixteen. Certainly way older than her actual age of twelve (*almost thirteen*).

She nervously checked around in the visible areas of the park but couldn't see anyone. After shuffling around for ten minutes, growing more uncomfortable and exposed, Mary texted Brad's mobile to check where he was.

No reply came and another five minutes rolled by.

As a last resort, Mary tried calling Brad on his mobile but it just went straight to voicemail. After another two minutes there had been no sign of Brad in person and no reply to any comms. As tears began to well up in Mary's pretty eyes, she started to make her way home.

When Mary walked in the front door of number twenty-eight, her mascara was smudged and her eyes were red and puffy. Cath jumped up, took her daughter into her arms and said, "Oh darlin', what's wrong?"

"I got stood up by a boy, on a first date," sobbed Mary. "I feel stupid and humiliated. I was sure he was going to be there," she continued with anger building inside her.

"Maybe something happened and he was delayed," countered Cath, knowing full well this was unlikely.

"He wasn't even answering his phone, text or call. I'm going to be a laughing stock, when people hear I got stood up."

Duncan had cottoned on to what had happened. He had slipped quietly onto the landing and heard everything.

Mary, you might not think it now but tonight, I reckon you've had a lucky escape.

Chapter 29

Mary had been so upset and distracted after Brad's no-show for their Friday night 'date', that she had abandoned her phone, switched on, downstairs. She had eventually cried herself to sleep in the early hours, detached from her phone, which was usually an extension of her arm.

By Saturday morning, the phone battery had drained to zero.

Mary had appeared downstairs around nine a.m. and noticed that Duncan was nowhere to be seen and her phone was 'dead'. Her mum was in the living room but kept her distance and didn't say anything, accepting that her daughter was hurting.

After Mary's phone had been on charge for a short time, the Glam Gang messages asking about last night had all started pinging her iPhone. The thought of telling them what happened filled her with dread. It had been bad enough confessing all to her mum but her peer group would be a whole other level.

After a few minutes of dithering, Mary accepted that she'd have to get her big girl pants on and face up to things. Mary didn't hint at any details but messaged her three pals to suggest a girls' gathering in Christina's café at eleven a.m. This would give her a decent time window to get her phone charged and steel herself for the ordeal of admitting she had been wrong about Brad.

She eventually got herself ready, didn't bother with make-up, threw her hair into a ponytail, then trudged wearily off to the meeting.

The other three friends were already seated in the café when Mary arrived, her downbeat demeanour suggesting things had not gone well with Brad.

As Mary sat in the empty seat at their table, Steph said, "Was it as bad as your face suggests?"

Mary was slightly shocked at Steph's directness but replied, "I got stood up... He was a no-show. I feel sooo humiliated after going on and on about how great he was." Mary stoically held off the tears, which weren't far away.

"What a scumbag. Did you try contacting him?" asked Di.

"Yes, of course. I got to the park just before half-seven but couldn't see anyone, not even a dog walker. I waited, texted him, waited some more and called his moby, but NOTHING. It was horrible. I felt really exposed just standing around, hoping for him to show up. I just wanted the ground to swallow me up. Eventually I went home, told my mum what had happened, it was just so mortifying. Our 'date' might have been a big joke to him but to me it was real."

Some 'date', thought Di, but didn't verbalise her opinion.

Mary was now into self-pity mode. "I'm such an idiot for believing him. Maybe I'm just a stupid wee lassie after all."

The other girls were feeling vindicated in their previous views but their friend looked thoroughly defeated.

"I could go down the 'told you so' route but you obviously

feel bad enough, so I'm not going to add salt to the wound. Life goes on, Mary. You deserve way better than him. It'll be fine in time, you'll see," said Ash, supportively.

As the four friends continued to talk, the Watcher was taking in their every movement and gesture, using his high-powered binoculars.

Yes, this group will provide the perfect pickings for me to have my revenge. These years of isolation and humiliation have made me stronger. I've got my modern-day toys to help me. This will need planning but I'll bide my time and I WILL have my day.

Mary was unaware of their stalker but was very aware that she'd lost a lot of group credibility with her stance on Brad and his ultimate non-appearance. She burned inside to redeem some status in the girls' group.

If I spill the details of the Haggi and Duncan, that'll put me right back in the game.

She then recalled Hannibal's reasoned warning from Monday night about maintaining secrecy; the potential fallout on her grandad's legacy, and impact on her brother and his new friends.

Mary swallowed her pride, kept her promise and said nothing.

By the time the girls headed for their respective homes, Mary felt a bit lighter, as they had not been as hard on her as she'd expected.

"See you on Monday at school," she said lamely as she started the walk for home.

As she neared the park on her route home, Haggi Hannibal suddenly appeared on a wall beside her, having come out of a bush. Mary jumped back in shock at his sudden appearance, having been lost in her own wee world.

"Psst, Mary, go tae the far bench in the park, behind the trees, we need tae show ye something."

Hannibal then disappeared.

Must be on the HSW again.

Mary gathered her wits about her, then strolled as casually as possible into the park and made her way over to the bench as asked.

The bench was in a secluded corner of the park, with restricted visibility, so there was less chance of being seen. Hannibal checked all around to make sure that the coast was clear, then himself and another Haggi started to 'bubble' on the bench beside her.

Mary was surprised to see a second wee, hairy being, one she wasn't familiar with.

"Mary – Sammy, Sammy – Mary," said Hannibal by way of introduction.

Sammy smiled a big friendly smile and said, "Hiya, Mary. Pleased tae meet ye."

Mary didn't react to her latest Haggi acquaintance.

Not wishing to drop Duncan in it with his sister, Hannibal explained, "Mary, dinnae git mad wi' us but we wir, anonymously, made aware o' this Brad guy a while back. Wu've been keeping tabs oan um, as we wanted tae check if thir wiz oany cause fir concern. Regrettably, there wiz 'n' is… cause fir concern, that is. Sammy and his Haggi partner, Punnet, huv been trackin' young Brad 'n' checking whit he's bin up tae. They made this bullet-point report fir the Haggi bigwigs. Huv a look."

Hannibal handed Mary a copy of report of the Monday to Wednesday previous, detailing Brad's illegal substance consumption and time with other girls. Her heart sank as she started to realise, she'd been played by Brad but through part bravado and part denial, she snapped, "My Brad isn't like that, you must have got it wrong."

Sammy then spoke in a slow, calm way, "Ah appreciate this isnae whit ye wannae hear, Mary, but Ah wiz there 'n' saw it aw wi' ma ain eyes."

He proceeded to give a detailed description of Brad's movements, who he was with and his 'activities'. Despite this further first-hand 'evidence', Mary was still hostile to believing what she was being told.

"I know you think you're helping here but trust me, you're not. I don't believe you guys, you're just trying to poison me against Brad."

Hannibal stayed silent for a few seconds then said, "OK, Mary, huv it yer ain waiy but we'll git mair proof if thit's whit it takes fur ye tae see the light. Whit reason dae we huv tae lie tae ye, given ye could blow oor cover in seconds? You need to trust us, this Brad is seriously BAD NEWS. So please stay away fae um 'n' oany o' his so-called pals."

What he says about 'no reason to lie' makes sense but I'm not listening to a couple of two-foot-tall fur balls.

Mary stood up and started to walk for home. She said over her shoulder, "Thanks for the advice, guys. See you around."

The two Haggi shook their heads despondently and watched Mary disappear out of the park.

Chapter 30

It was Sunday, mid-afternoon and Brad 'Casanova' Thomas was breathing deeply. As he lay, semi-conscious, on his bed, he had no idea he'd been asleep for almost two full days.

The Haggi Berry Brew had wreaked a terrible revenge.

A little earlier Brad had stirred, very briefly, with a crashing sore head. His throat had felt as if someone had hoovered all the moisture out of it with a Dyson. He had just groaned and gone straight back to sleep.

His mother, in spite of being somewhat drunk herself, was concerned. Concerned that her young son seemed to have been crashed out, probably drunk, for an awfully long time. Although he was two years under the legal drinking age, this never occurred to her. She did, to be fair, act like a concerned adult and called the emergency services to explain the situation.

It took four hours for an ambulance to arrive. The paramedics asked what had happened and other core details. She had replied, as best she could, but didn't add much of value.

The trained medical staff did the standard checks on Brad plus blood pressure, ECG and tox screens. Despite fairly extensive checks, they could find no medical reason or explanation for sleeping for two days. Other than a blood-alcohol reading, which was about as high as the paramedics had ever seen, even after *forty-eight hours* of sleep.

Brad would be dehydrated when he surfaced, so the paramedics urged that, once he did, he keep drinking lots of water. All should be fine but, if not, phone NHS 24.

No sooner had the paramedics left the street, than the front door opened and a heavily lived-in face, looked out. Brad's mum went down the path with as much purpose as she could muster, in her current, hazy state. She cut a sad and desperate figure as she rocked her way, on stick-like legs, to the corner shop. It was a big effort for her to walk, but nothing was more important than topping up her vodka and wine supply. She'd also decided to add a couple of bottles of water to her purchases, for Brad.

As Brad's mum went out of sight on her shopping trip, the Haggi duo of Sammy and Punnet were watching from a nearby tree. They jumped down, pushed the half-closed front door open, and went to pay Brad his follow-up visit.

Sammy set off to check where Casanova Brad was sleeping. Meanwhile, Punnet went into the kitchen for a snoop around.

They briefly met up in the hallway.

Sammy confirmed Brad was asleep in his room and Punnet dropped the bombshell that there was a 'creature that cannot be named', i.e. a cat, in the kitchen.

"Time for fireworks," said Sammy as he took a quick sip of HSW, became invisible and went back into the kitchen.

Sammy stood about three feet in front of the allergy monster. As Sammy was invisible, the cat could see nothing but sensed there was a presence nearby and went on the alert.

Suddenly, there was a huge allergic sneeze from Sammy.

The cat screeched and jumped straight up in the air, like a jump-jet aircraft, then landed back on all fours.

Bubbles started to appear as Sammy's invisibility began to wear off. As Sammy became fully visible, he shouted, "Ya mangy moggie, we're here tae mess wi' yer mind."

The hyped up cat flicked out its claws, arched its back, hissed viciously then went into full psycho mode. As the deranged feline made this manoeuvre, its tail flipped up and pointed straight at the ceiling.

Quick as a flash, from out of the cat's vision, Punnet squirted chilli oil, which he'd got from the cupboard, right up the cat's butthole. The cat had been primed for murder previously but once the heat of the chilli oil kicked in, it was in rocket launch to the moon mode. The frenzied cat leapt onto the worktop and started writhing around, frantically trying to cushion or cool its burning butt. Utensils and pans went flying everywhere, cupboard doors flew open and crockery started bouncing around wildly.

Smashing, banging and crashing.

The sound in the enclosed space was deafening.

Without any notice, both laughing Haggi took a sip of their magic water and simply vanished. The demented cat was nonplussed for a second or two at their sudden disappearance.

The desperate fur ball then sprang out of the partly open kitchen window, pulling the voile curtain with it as it went.

Brad Thomas finally woke up to what sounded like a scalded cat on acid with a Red Bull chaser and wielding a large baseball bat.

The high-pitched squealing and wrecking ball sounds

stopped, suddenly.

A pressing pain in his stomach indicated a desperate need to pee. He moved, as quickly as he could, to the nearby toilet.

He stood in front of the pan with the lid and seat up and looked forward with relish, to the upcoming relief flow. He did start to pee but the yellow liquid didn't reach the pan. It bounced, splattered and squirted all over the toilet, on the walls, on the floor and back onto him. The age-old 'cling film over the pan' trick had claimed another victim.

The two invisible Haggi came from the kitchen battle with the cat and into the small toilet. They had to work very hard to stifle their laughter at the cling film prank.

Brad then got his serious talking to, as he started to hear voices.

"Lassies seem tae think yer God's gift but in reality yer jist a nasty, wee stoner, giein' thum bevvy 'n' takin' pure advantage," said Sammy for openers.

Brad hardly registered the words as he flailed around, trying to wipe up his stray pee with toilet roll.

"If they could only see ye noo," Sammy continued with a gleeful look on his face.

Despite the ludicrous toilet scene, Brad now seemed to have greater awareness that a serious message was being delivered to him.

Sammy finished off his speech. "We've warned ye already tae quit yer nonsense so wur tellin' ye again, quit messin' lasses aroond 'n' bein' a creep. Take this as a final telling. Keep away fae Mary McPherson or in the words ay Arnie, *WE'LL BE BACK*. If ye go near her, yir pee will nay jist be squirting everywhere… ye might nae huv oanythin' tae squirt wi'. Git ma drift?"

To emphasise the final threat, a Haggi dagger appeared in front of Brad private parts. As he glanced down and saw the free-floating dagger, Brad passed out and collapsed on the pee-covered floor.

Two minutes later, Brad's mother returned from the corner shop with her liquid bounty. As she opened the front door, the house-wrecking Haggi duo slipped past her, unseen. They skipped down the stairs, nodded to each other and said simultaneously, "Hagg-nificent joab, ma man."

A few seconds later Brad's mum registered the chaos in the kitchen and toilet, screamed, and then phoned the emergency services for the second time that day.

Chapter 31

After the girls' café meeting, Mary had been tetchy with Duncan and Cath for the remainder of Sunday.

Mary had collared Duncan in his room at one point and told him, "Hannibal's been bending my ear about staying away from Brad. I'm not giving up on him that easily, there might still be a perfectly good reason he didn't show for our 'date'. I'm getting seriously hacked off with your wee, hairy friends. And don't think that I can't work out who the anonymous tipster was. Hannibal tried to cover it up but I'm sure it was you."

Mary then stomped off in a foul mood.

"Just trying to look out for you, sis. Someone has to," called Duncan after her, knowing it wouldn't make any difference.

The following school week was relatively uneventful, although there were some interesting developments, mostly away from school. Brad did not make school on the Monday morning after his Sunday follow-up visit from Sammy and Punnet. By Tuesday, however, young Brad resumed his previous activities. While not making any contact with Mary, he did have a few 'dates' arranged. Brad's brain must have been more fogged up than he realised. He had somehow forgotten having a knife waved in front of his privates and the warnings from the Haggi.

Brad had three consecutive evening liaisons in the park, all with different girls. Two of these girls travelled by bus, from other towns, taken in by tales and photos of the beautiful bad boy of Auchterbarn.

The Thomas family cat had not been seen since Sunday.

Ms Robinson continued to act like a dedicated and valuable teacher, with her class more enthused and engaged than she could have dreamed. Duncan's hero rep from recent times dropped off from its height but he and Davy had a new found respected status. They still kept themselves to themselves but life was much more pleasant and less stressful.

Thursday and Friday was when things got interesting.

During Thursday, at Auchterbarn Secondary School, it was advised that there would be a Gala Week announcement in Friday's assembly. This set the rumour mill alive with speculation of what would be announced for the early summer festival week.

On the Thursday evening, teacher Rowena Robinson attended her first Alcoholics Anonymous (AA) meeting. While full of trepidation, with the support of Jocky Pearson, her fellow teacher, Rowena stood up and told her tale to a group of people, who had all walked her walk. By the time she drove home, stone cold sober, Duncan's teacher felt like a weight had been removed and that the future could certainly be brighter.

That same night, the Haggi cameras and microphones in Grange Park had recorded the third night in a row of Brad's encounters. The footage gave the Haggi all the confirmation and ammunition they needed.

The Senior Council were consulted and shown the video and audio of the last few days. While not prone to emotional decision making, they were filled with anger and frustration that Brad had not heeded two previous warnings and remained a threat to local girls.

He's been well warned and chosen to ignore the Haggi – WRONG MOVE, MATE.

The Haggi elders sanctioned Brad's demise by very modern communication methods. Big Tony burned the midnight oil, edited the park footage, saved the files to his laptop and travelled by Hagg-mobile in the wee hours of Friday morning. His destination was another town and the property of a Connected family, so that he could use their internet connection to mask the Haggi involvement.

Their niece had been one of the unfortunate girls that fell for the lure of Brad Thomas, so they were very invested in ensuring he got payback. In the early hours of Friday, a personalised message and a collection of recent 'Brad videos' was sent to Mary. The videos were date and time stamped and the sound and picture quality were high. So was Brad most of the time.

Brad's behaviour, in the videos, was more or less a carbon copy of the report submitted by Sammy and Punnet, i.e. teen girls, illegal substances and inappropriate behaviour. Not only was Mary sent the videos directly but fake 'Schoolgirl Scorned' accounts had been set up on various platforms.

Brad's videos were posted all across social media and a copy sent to the local police.

His reign as the Auchterbarn heartthrob was obliterated, there and then.

Chapter 32

Cath's Friday morning wake-up shout woke Mary from a sound sleep. She instinctively picked up her iPhone, which had been plugged in and charging overnight on the side table, as she got out of bed and headed for the bathroom.

Though still somewhat sleepy, Mary noticed more than a dozen new text and voice messages from her girls' inner circle but there was also an email message headed up, *Bad Boy Brad – Mary you need to see this.*

After a quick toilet visit and washing her hands, Mary returned to the haven of her own room to check out the mysterious message. She was a bit suspicious of an email from an unknown source but, given the title and recent events, she impatiently opened the message.

As well as the heading, there were multiple video attachments and a few words of supporting text.

Mary,

We know you are struggling to accept that Brad is bad news for you (and others).

We hope that the attached videos will convince you to believe that what we've been telling you is the truth.

The footage from the park is 100% genuine.
Regards,
Your Invisible Friends
P.S. The videos have also been posted across multiple social media platforms and passed on to the local police but you are not mentioned anywhere.

Mary was initially filled with fury that the Haggi were messing in her affairs AGAIN and thoughts of 'outing' them were running amok in her mind. She was close to going to seek out Duncan and making a huge scene but intrigue got the better of her and she pressed play on the first attachment.

The video was of very good quality and timestamped at seven-twenty-five p.m. on the immediately passed Tuesday evening. The views cut between three different camera locations in Grange Park, which Mary recognised from the footage.

Brad was seated alone on a secluded park bench, near the tree line on the far side. The local Romeo was clearly swigging straight vodka from a bottle, which he picked up from under the bench. He was intermittently smoking a spliff but was still aware enough to notice a new arrival.

A nervous-looking, dark-haired teenage girl, whom Mary recognised as a second year from their school, walked through the park gate. Mary got a fright as the sound of Brad's voice, on the video, clearly called, "Over here, doll, come and join the party."

The teenage girl made her way over towards where Brad was seated and as she reached the bench, he beckoned her to sit, with a sweep of his hand. Mary didn't know the girl's name but her dislike for her was immediate, as Brad had showed up for her, unlike for Mary previously.

There was a little chat between the two inhabitants of the park bench and Brad offered the girl a drink of vodka from the bottle. She didn't look very comfortable but Mary could understand why she would drink it to appear grown up and fit in.

The drinking continued plus offers of smoking. The girl tried to smoke a little but recoiled after her first 'drag', then looked like she was going to be sick. Brad gave her some time to recover from the smoking attempt and, after a few more swigs of vodka, moved in closer and started to kiss the girl, who initially responded.

The contact quickly became more intense and the teenage girl becoming more agitated through the next few minutes. She eventually managed to escape Brad's clutches, shouting, "I said no," then stood up, straightened her clothing and hair, then quickly headed for the park entrance.

Brad didn't flinch, just stayed on the bench and continued to drink and smoke, making no effort to even look round to follow the girl's progress out of Grange Park.

Mary stopped the video, feeling uneasy at what she'd just seen but the devil on her shoulder was urging her to watch further videos. After about a minute of deliberation, she gave in to her urge and watched the others as well.

The second and third videos were similar in content to the first, with girls of a similar age 'visiting' Brad. The variance in the later videos was that the girls were blonde, from another school and Mary didn't recognise them. The girl in the second video, from Wednesday, looked, and proved to be more comfortable and experienced, generally. She partook in all the drinking and smoking and also didn't reject Brad, at any point, during their romp on the bench.

The girl in the third video from Thursday had reacted more like the girl from Tuesday during the bench activities, eventually screaming and kneeing Brad in the bollocks before bolting for the exit.

By the time Mary stopped the third video, any lingering positive feelings she had towards Brad were long gone and she didn't doubt that the footage was genuine.

Three different girls on three consecutive nights – he's a player and I've been played like a fiddle. I've been wrong, all along, defending him but he's just a creepy chancer and the others have been right. My cred is ruined because of that scumbag. I hate him.

Mary knew there was no way she could face the girls at school today, after these video revelations, so when Cath gave her a second chase-up call, she turned on the amateur dramatics. Cath came up the stairs, knocked and opened Mary's bedroom door to find her still in pyjamas and looking as miserable as her acting could convey. Mary had even gone as far as dabbing some water, from the glass beside her bed, onto her forehead to make it look like she was sweating and burning up.

"What's up, Mary?"

"I just feel really hot and flu-ey... like someone's taken my batteries out... I've no energy."

Cath bought the sob story. "Oh all right, Mary, stay in your bed and don't go in to school, it's only the one day. I've got to go to work, so you'll have to look after yourself till I'm home. There's bread and some bits in the fridge for lunch, if you're up to it. Remember, I don't want any reports of 'sightings' of you out and about. Do you hear me?"

"Loud and clear, I'm not going anywhere," replied Mary quietly, in her best pathetic-sounding voice.

Mary heard the front door closing as her mum went off to work and Duncan to school. She waited a couple of minutes to make sure they were gone for good, then turned her attention to the Glam Gang messages and the online comments, on the back of the Brad videos going out on social media.

The comments from various people mirrored a lot of what was going through Mary's mind.

Stoner Scumbag

Dodged a bullet M.

What an absolute creep, no respect.

Patter stinks, mate.

Poor lassie doesn't look like she wants to be there and can't get away quick enough.

OMG – Wednesday lassie will be a mum by 16 (if that)!

Girls are nothing to this guy, just a challenge to see how far he can get. He is sexy though!

Same crappy chat and M.O. every night.

How pathetic calling them all 'doll'. Likely does this to avoid getting any names wrong and getting caught out by his harem!

There were some typical lads' comments such as 'good on ye, mate, get what you can' but generally the comments were fairly scathing towards Brad.

After a few minutes Mary dropped her phone on the bed and slumped down into the duvet. She knew she should respond to the Glam Gang messages but couldn't face it.

By school morning break time, more messages came in from the Gang. These were sympathetic, rather than 'told you so' and the girls just wanted to make sure that Mary was OK, as much as anything else. They confirmed that the Gala Week announcements had been made and it was confirmed that Steph had been voted Gala Queen, narrowly beating Mary to the role.

Oh, great, I'm such a loser that I didn't get the Gala Queen role either. Probably lost out due to this Brad disaster.

Another thing confirmed for the Gala Week Saturday, was that the lorry float drivers would all dress as superheroes, to enhance the spectacle. In addition, the organisers announced a big concert with a mystery but substantial 'headline' artist. This was to take place on a specially constructed stage on the football pitches, after the Gala parade. The concert would act as the grand finale and supplement the stalls, shows and kids' entertainment on the big day.

Mary eventually summoned up the courage and texted her Glam Gang pals. She explained that she had 'skived off' school, faking illness, but needed time to process the video revelations and the implications. There was no direct mention of the Brad social media content but Mary acknowledged and thanked them for their various messages of support. She also magnanimously congratulated Steph on her selection as Queen.

Through a series of texts, a further girls' meet at Christina's café was agreed for the next morning.

By the time Cath and Duncan returned home from their respective establishments, in the late afternoon, Mary was dressed and sitting in the living room. She said she was feeling better and helped Cath to make the dinner. A quiet family Friday night in followed and Mary's morning illness was a thing of the past.

By ten thirty-five on the Saturday morning, the Glam Gang were seated around a rectangular table in Christina's café. They'd been there for five minutes, with Mary arriving last of the four. There had been some minor small talk but things were VERY awkward between Mary and the others, especially Steph. While Mary had congratulated her on being elected Gala Queen by text, as they sat, face to face across the table, there was still simmering frustration flowing from Mary in waves.

Even people sitting nearby could feel the tension amongst the group of girls.

Eventually Steph couldn't hold her frustration any further and said, "Mary, we've been pals forever, I just need to say this. I'm really chuffed to be elected as Gala Queen and feel like a winner for once. I'm not going to apologise for winning or being happy about it. I'm sorry that you missed out but the organisers did recognise that it was REALLY close, so they created a role for you. We'll both be on the main Royal float and be able to enjoy the day, together."

"What is the role?"

"Best Maid to the Queen."

"Wow, not only do I not get to be Queen, I get offered a servant's role instead. Thanks but no thanks, I'd rather stay at home," replied Mary, bitterly.

"Harsh, Mary, very harsh. Not your finest hour," said Di.

Ash was red faced and looked fit to burst, as she added her tuppence worth. "Stop and listen to yourself, Miss High and Mighty. You're getting all humpty about narrowly coming second and moaning about being offered a secondary role, when some of us mere mortals never even received one single vote. Suck it up, get over yourself and back into the real world. We just want the old Mary back."

Mary was a bit stunned and stewed silently for several minutes. The others held their silence and nerve, not reacting or moving a muscle.

As she reflected on Ash's comments and the wisdom of Hannibal's previous speech about loyalty and relationships, Mary came to the realisation that she really wanted, and needed, to be back in the comfort bubble of their unified friends group.

She softened her posture, took a breath, then spoke. "Look, guys, I now realise I've been a real bitch over all this Brad stuff. It's me that's caused all the unnecessary drama and I've been all 'me, me, me', when all you've done is be supportive, even when I couldn't see the wood for the trees. I'm sorry to you all, whether it's my hormones... stubborn stupidity... self-destructive tendencies, whatever... I just don't want to fight anymore and I'd like my friends back, with no more drama. By way of apology, the drinks are on me. What do you fancy?"

"Perhaps not the best wording, given your fancy caused all this friction in the first place," commented Di, perceptively.

The four friends started to laugh and the mood instantly lightened. Mary took the drinks orders and they all helped to get them back to the table, along with a selection of muffins.

A lengthy, open and healthy discussion about the Brad videos, boys in general, recent events and the upcoming Gala Week took place. Mary agreed to support Steph and be Best Maid to her Queen.

Great debate was held around who would be the headline concert act, with some fairly wild suggestions being put forward.

Smiles and laughter prevailed and the Glam Gang were reunited in harmony.

Chapter 33

Over the last fortnight, the Watcher had been busy finalising his research and planning. He'd walked the town as inconspicuously as possible, familiarising the layout and places of note and interest, plus read the local press and kept up to date on various social media channels. He was therefore, well-versed regarding the upcoming Gala Week events and the demise of Romeo Brad.

I can scarcely believe how recent events have fallen into place to aid my plan.

The mystery man had gleaned that two of his four possible Glam Gang 'options' (Steph AND Mary) would be involved in official Gala Week roles. Even better, they'd likely be travelling on the same vehicle in the main Gala parade through the town.

Steph's dad is the retired football guy, who must be fairly minted given his career and the fancy big house they live in. Mary's dad George is a highly successful architect with a thriving business. He's also bought a new mansion with his dolly-dimple girlfriend, so he must be good for cash too. I don't think £100,000 each would be too onerous and fairly easy to raise, in short order, for wealthy individuals like them.

He knew he'd need to keep checking and planning but

things were looking good for the Watcher.

I WILL have my day and once the daddies pay up, I can disappear with plenty of cash to last a while.

The Watcher re-watched the Brad Thomas' video clips and reviewed the follow-up comments. He had various negative views on the whole debacle but restricted his thoughts.

Stupid, gullible, naive wee lassies, who think they're the bees knees and know it all. Really!!!

In light of the Haggi video distribution, Brad Thomas's local credibility was zero, so he had cut his losses and quit school. He was rumoured to have left home, looking for pastures new and a fresh start.

The nights continued to lengthen as the Gala Week preparations continued apace. Work was ongoing on the design and construction of the various lorry float sets and stages for the big day. Designated float drivers were getting their costumes together but maintaining a wall of secrecy on their superhero identities.

Secrecy also remained over the headline Gala Concert but a couple of up and coming local bands had been announced as the warm-up acts.

Chapter 34

It was Friday, early June and the day before the Gala parade and concert.

As Duncan walked into class after the lunch break, he noticed Ms Robinson deep in thought. "Everything OK, Miss? You look miles away," asked Duncan.

"Oh, sorry Duncan, I'm just back from the shops and I saw this guy. It's been bothering me but can't put my finger on why. He's just an ordinary bloke but that's now three times that I've seen him, recently. Definitely not a local but seems vaguely familiar from somewhere. He has a purple birthmark on the left side of his face and, weirdly, it's shaped almost exactly like a map of Cyprus. I know that, as my dad served there when he was in the services. He often brought things back for Mum with Cyprus stuff on them. She had a dish towel with the Cyprus island map on it, I can see it like it was yesterday."

Ms Robinson picked up her phone, ran a search for a map of Cyprus and showed it to Duncan. He thought she had finally lost the plot but said, "Useful to know," just for something to say.

The afternoon ran without further incident at the primary

school and by the time Duncan walked home with Davy, he had forgotten all about the mystery man with the birthmark.

Half a mile away in Auchterbarn Secondary, Steph and Mary were working with the drama teacher to get their final adjustments made on their outfits for tomorrow's parade. Mary had accepted her lesser role and only needed a couple of minor things done. Steph was having her Royal gown slightly reworked.

The reworking was unnecessary as Steph looked fabulous in her outfit but she was revelling in her glorious 'moment in the sun'.

The school day finished as the bell went for home time.

Both girls were happy with their outfits, which were carefully hung up, so as to be perfect for the big day. As they went their separate ways to go home, Mary said, "See you at yours about ten to start getting ready. Can't wait."

She surprised herself in saying this last bit but genuinely meant it.

"Cheers, M, see you then," replied Steph, still glowing at the prospect of being the centre of attention tomorrow.

The Saturday Gala morning arrived with a very welcome bright sun, light winds and a mostly blue sky. The weather forecast was for more of the same, all day, so no brollies or jackets would be needed by spectators and participants alike.

Mary and Steph were in the Findlay house, busy getting their appearances just right, for their public at the Gala Parade. Relations between them were much improved since the 'clear the air' discussion in the café and they chatted excitedly as they had done for years.

"I'm so glad that I stopped being so bitchy and we get to do this together today," said Mary.

"Me too, it wouldn't have felt the same if you weren't part of it. You are my bestie after all."

They finally emerged from Steph's bedroom to admiring glances from Steph's mum and dad.

Maggie Findlay told her daughter how beautiful she looked and complimented Mary too, with a tear in her eye. Steph's proud dad, Bryan, was too emotional to speak in the house so hurried out to the car to take up his chauffeur duties, before he embarrassed himself.

The girls walked regally down the steps into Bryan's waiting car and he drove them to their school to get their outfits, then onward to the east end of Main Street to join the Royal float.

Chapter 35

The Gala Parade was scheduled to start at two p.m. Flatbed float lorries were to assemble, in the order provided to drivers in advance, at one forty-five p.m. at the east end of Main Street. The Royal float was the final vehicle in the procession, so would be best to arrive last to join the line.

The Watcher had done his homework and the driver of the 'Royal' float had long since been identified. Every detail about him had been checked and memorised. His name was Jimmy Brown, a retired local man in his late sixties, who had driven lorry floats in the Gala parade for years.

At twenty past one, Jimmy emerged from his bungalow, onto the pavement, in a full Superman costume. He had worked hard to keep his superhero choice secret, so it would only be revealed today. He planned to walk the short distance to the lorry park and collect his 'Royal' float lorry, to join the parade line-up.

Just as Jimmy was closing his garden gate, Spider-Man (AKA the Watcher) timed his approach perfectly, his face hidden under the full coverage of his costume mask.

"Howdy, Clark," as in Kent, Superman's alter ego. "What

float are you driving today?" said the Watcher, jokingly, knowing full well what the answer would be.

"I'm on Royal Float duties today, centre of attention, just heading for the lorry park to pick it up now," replied Jimmy, proudly.

"Good for you. I'm just heading to the car park to pick up my float too. You have remembered the keys for your lorry, haven't you?" enquired Spider-Man, as he quickly surveyed the area for any prying eyes.

"Of course, got them here," said Superman Jimmy, waving the lorry keys to demonstrate he had them.

Spider-Man took a step forward, as if to start walking to the lorry park, then faked a stumble and groaned. Jimmy bent down to go to assist but, quick as a flash, he was put in a headlock, pulled to the ground and hit hard on the head with a blunt object.

Five minutes later, not so Superman, Jimmy, was bound and gagged in his own garden shed. The emboldened Spider-Man made sure he wasn't seen leaving the premises and walked off confidently, lorry keys in hand, to drive the Royal float in the parade.

The Watcher walked the short distance to the lorry park, opened up the 'Royal' vehicle and sat, contentedly, in the driver's seat. He deliberately didn't catch the eye of, or speak to any other drivers, simply bided his time till all the other vehicles had left, then set off to bring up the rear of the long line.

By one forty-five p.m. all lorries were in line and ready as the drivers had been instructed. There was no indication, at all, that anything was amiss.

Bryan Findlay pulled up to drop the girls off for their big

moment. He stopped his car near the line of lorries and went round to open the doors for the Queen and her Best Maid. He helped them out, one at a time, and felt a huge wave of emotion sweep over him as Steph stepped out, looking a million dollars.

My beautiful princess.

Bryan proudly kissed Steph, wished the girls all the best for the parade then went to park his car and meet up with his wife Maggie, who was tasked with securing a good vantage point on Main Street.

Once up the steps and aboard the 'Royal' lorry, Steph and Mary were so excited, waving to all and sundry, that they paid no attention to the superhero in the driver's seat of their vehicle. The girls took a couple of selfies on their phones then surveyed the manic scenes of last-minute arrivals and adjustments to the sets on the floats.

The minutes ticked by quickly and it was soon two p.m.

Mary, in her role as Best Maid, escorted Queen Steph to her throne and placed the 'Royal' crown on her friend's head. She then took her own seat, a little to the side. There they were, two long-time friends, alone on stage, enjoying the limelight.

Mary was still a little jealous that she wasn't on the throne but was happy that if it wasn't her, it was her bestie.

As the lorries in the parade started their engines and crawled forward to start proceedings, the Watcher was happily smiling under his sweat-inducing, but vital Spider-Man mask.

All going to plan so far.

Bryan managed to find a parking place on a busy side street and joined his wife Maggie in a good viewing spot on Main Street. Cath McPherson was already there, chatting excitedly with Maggie, and their mobiles were primed for capturing the parade as it passed. A reluctantly attending Duncan was stood close by, doing his best to look enthused. George was with Marlene, further along on the other side of Main Street to avoid meeting the other parents.

The murmurs of discussion amongst the large crowds increased, as the line of lorry floats came slowly into view. It must have taken about twenty-five minutes for a mix of all the floats, a pipe band, other musical accompaniment and multiple performers on foot, to pass by.

Parents and friends waved at the floats and participants as they strove to identify their family members or pals. Cath and Maggie both managed to capture excellent video and photos of the parade with the core focus on the 'Royal' vehicle as it passed.

As the Royal vehicle passed the end of Main Street the number of spectators reduced significantly as everyone headed off. The scramble was on towards the stage on the local football pitches, to try to secure a good vantage point for the upcoming concert.

The lorries were to be parked up in a designated car park but as the 'Royal' float was last, it would be expected to be the last one back to the parking place.

This was what the Watcher was relying on.

The line of parade vehicles had travelled well beyond Main Street. The first couple of lorries were starting to turn towards the designated car park area, which was close to the football fields, the concert stage and the various entertainment options.

Having checked that no spectators were visible, Spider-Man slowed to let the other vehicles get further ahead. He deliberately botched a noisy gear change, to make it appear there was an issue, then stalled the lorry intentionally.

He got out and quickly moved round to the back of the lorry, where the girls were still seated on the thrones and wondering what had happened.

Their fun day, very quickly became anything but fun.

The girls were initially relaxed and amused as Spider-Man sprang up onto the flatbed trailer. This changed to looks of horror and fear as their previously unnoticed driver brandished a large knife and a yellow handheld object that looked like a gun.

"Not a peep or a false move from either of you or you get hurt, REAL BAD. This here is a Taser gun, which can do TERRIBLE damage. If one of you moves or makes a sound, then the other one gets it. Understood?"

The two terrified pals said nothing but nodded agreement, as the Watcher took a roll of tape from a backpack, while still pointing the Taser at his victims. He covered their mouths in turn, with tape, and also bound their hands.

The girls were then ushered into the off-side of the driver's cab, made to huddled together and duck down out of sight. Spider-Man bound their bodies and legs in more tape so they were joined together in the cramped, dirty and stinky space.

The Watcher wrapped scarves around their heads and tied these, so they acted as blindfolds. He then used the remote key lock to secure the door, while he got round to the driver's side.

The lorry engine came to life as the friends realised they were in serious trouble but at least they had each other and weren't dealing with this alone.

The kidnapper initially drove carefully, sticking to the speed limit and watching the tied-up duo like a hawk. After a couple of minutes, as almost the entire town were heading for the football fields, the kidnapper realised there was zero traffic and very limited risk of being seen.

My plan and timing have been spot on.

He accelerated up to the maximum speed the lorry was capable of and made for his storage location, where the girls would be held captive.

Mary concentrated on the motion of the lorry as best she could, given how uncomfortable they were. They drove on a smooth surface for a few minutes, bumped along for a bit, then stopped, suddenly, no more than three or four miles from town, she estimated.

The girls were bundled out of the lorry, falling in a heap on the dusty ground, making a mess of their Gala Day outfits.

This was the least of their issues at this stage.

A few minutes later the girls were bound, gagged and blindfolded back to back in a remote location, while Spider-Man drove the lorry speedily back to town. He breathed deeply while he drove, still clad in his full Spider-Man costume and mask.

There were only a few disinterested stragglers heading to the football pitches when the 'Royal' lorry pulled in and parked up in the designated lorry park.

This will throw them off the scent for a while.

Spider-Man switched off the engine and scanned all around the area for any witnesses. No one was nearby and the few people he saw were otherwise engaged, so he jumped down from the lorry and made his way away from the area.

As he had rehearsed, the kidnapper walked to a well-hidden area in the nearby trees and removed his costume, which he put in his backpack rather than discarding it and leaving evidence. He was back in his lightweight black clothing as he started walking, back to where he'd left the captive girls. This was also part of his plan to avoid his car being seen in the area or on CCTV cameras.

As the kidnapper left the town, the two terrified girls were trying unsuccessfully to communicate and free themselves.

Duncan had long since excused himself and headed home when Cath asked Maggie, "Have you heard from Steph?"

The mothers had got a decent spot to watch the concert and were keeping an eye out for the girls to catch their attention.

"No. Anything from Mary to you?"

"Not a dicky bird but I thought they'd be off the float and here by now. You stay here and keep our space, Maggie, and I'll go and check if the 'Royal' float is back in the lorry park," said Cath, and off she went to have a look.

When Cath got to the lorry park, the float that the girls had travelled on was parked up with the throne and stage all still in place. There was no sign of the driver or, more importantly, the girls.

Cath phoned Mary's mobile, which was turned off, and she then called Maggie.

The Findlays had had no luck in finding or contacting Steph either.

Alarm bells were now ringing and panic set in as Cath ran back to the football field area, grabbed Maggie and the two of them found a police officer near the concert stage. They breathlessly explained that they couldn't locate their daughters, there was no way they had disappeared voluntarily and something bad was likely to have happened.

The officer tried to stem their fears and calm them both

down but the two mothers were becoming increasingly worried and frantic. Despite desperate searches and police checks there was no sign anywhere of the Gala Queen and her Best Maid.

The girls were gone, presumably taken against their will.

An announcement of the girls' disappearance was made over the stage sound system and the headline concert cancelled, as everyone turned their focus to finding the missing girls.

Chapter 36

The McPherson and Findlay parents were understandably distraught at their girls being kidnapped in plain sight. The police had set up an incident room at the local police station and advised the parents that as many resources as possible were being made available.

There had still been no major leads since the abductions. Further media appeals had been made for any witnesses to come forward.

Emotions were running high but after discussions with the police, and between themselves, the four parents had decided to use the Findlay family home in Auchterbarn as a base. They would all stay there as much as possible, while the girls were being looked for, so that it was simpler to keep them all up to speed with developments and make any decisions.

Duncan had insisted on staying in the McPherson house, in his own bed. Cath was concerned that he, too, might be targeted and was opposed to his idea. However, after a few minutes of debate, she was in such emotional turmoil that eventually she agreed.

Duncan isn't good with change or unusual surroundings. As long as everything is locked tight, I'll let him be.

The existing relationship chasm between Cath and George had not narrowed in the hours since the kidnapping but they maintained a degree of civility for public appearance's sake.

All four parents had considered going out searching for the girls but, in the end, accepted they didn't have the skills and would be best to leave the search to the police. This didn't stop them discussing various wide-ranging theories and possibilities and sleep was only fleeting, if had at all.

Marlene was so concerned about George's daughter being kidnapped, that she'd spent two hours shopping online.

The kidnapper, meanwhile, was wise enough to know that any phone call would be intercepted and recorded by the police. This eliminated this method of ransom demand from his calculations.

Through his months of planning and stalking the girls, the kidnapper knew the family properties and surrounding areas exceptionally well. He knew he was taking a big risk but under darkness in the early hours of Sunday morning, his ransom demand was made. Hand-delivered notes were put through Cath's house door, George's door and a third to the Findlay house.

The demand was typed on plain paper with full details of an overseas bank account detailed on a separate sheet.

The girls are safe but you need to comply to keep it that way.

The police are NOT to be advised of anything connected to the ransom demand.

Dire consequences await your girls if you breach this condition.

£50,000 is to be transferred overseas, up front, to demonstrate goodwill (see account details on separate sheet).

It's a shell company account and untraceable, so don't even try to locate me through this.

Funds to be in the overseas account by close of business on Tuesday.

A further £150,000 in cash is to be available on Thursday at a time and drop point to be advised.

I have access to modern technology and weapons and will use them if required.

A drone will be watching you and the cash drop zone so no police or funny business.

Play nice and you get your girls back unharmed.

There had been no sleep for any of the four worried parents and they had largely remained congregated in the kitchen, praying for a positive update. Other than sharing wild theories and occasional toilet breaks, nothing much had happened.

A police liaison officer had been assigned and was due to arrive around eight a.m. Around seven-thirty Maggie had decided to go upstairs to get a shower and change her clothes. As she went towards the stairs, her eye caught something white, lying on the ground inside the front door. She rushed over and picked up two sheets of paper, stapled together and folded into thirds.

As she started to unfold the paper, her heart sank as she realised it was a ransom note. She immediately shouted out and ran back through to the others.

Bryan took it on himself to read the note aloud to the others. "Definitely a kidnapping then. This is like a really bad movie," he said.

"At least we know what happened, but how do we handle this now? It says no police but a police liaison officer is arriving any minute," added Cath.

"I reckon we keep the ransom request quiet but if there is

actually a drone, he's going to see our new arrival very soon. I just want the girls back safely," added Maggie.

"In terms of the up-front fifty thousand, how do we raise that?" enquired Bryan.

"I've not got much spare cash," said George, immediately going on the financial defensive.

"OK then, I'll pay this up front money as we've got more than that amount in our account. You can just pay a higher share of the balance, George. I don't care about the money, I just want our Princess back safe," said a tearful Bryan Findlay.

The four highly stressed parents went on to debate how to proceed plus smaller details, including:-
- Getting proof that the girls were alive before paying any money over.
- More than one person involved/kidnapper accomplices?
- How can one person operate a drone and pick up the money?
- Is the drone a bluff?
- Who could do this?
- Is he local?
- How was the ransom note delivered?
- Where might the girls be? Anywhere nearby?
- Police – yes or no?

They felt powerless and frustrated as the doorbell was rung by the liaison officer.

Chapter 37

The Haggi jungle drums had made HHHQ aware of the kidnapping of Mary and Steph.

At four-fifteen a.m. on the Sunday morning it still wasn't properly light as Duncan was wakened by a bump on his shoulder. He opened his eyes sleepily and practically jumped out of his skin, as Haggi Hannibal was standing on the bed beside him.

"Time tae git up 'n' movin', Dunc. Ah got in thru the open windae. Wur organisin' a search fur the girls. Handy 'n' an auld Haggi tracking expert called Sniffer ur oan the case. Me, you 'n' the warrior posse ur to meet at the car park where the lorries wur left, eftir the Gala parade. Come oan, shift yer erse," urged Hannibal, grumpily.

Duncan wearily got dressed and locked up the house as Hannibal zoomed ahead to the rendezvous on his Hagg-mobile.

It took Duncan twenty minutes to walk to the lorry car park, which wasn't a 'proper' car park with tarmac. It was just hard-packed dirt mixed with gravel and was usually used by tour buses or bigger lorries, thus avoiding traffic congestion in the Main Street. This car park was where the Gala vehicles, including the Gala Queen float, had been brought after the parade.

It was almost fully light by the time Duncan arrived on scene. There were no humans or traffic around, so the Haggi were taking a chance in being visible, while looking for tracking clues. They were, however, eagle-eyed and had their Haggi Special Water at the ready in case anyone raised an alarm.

Duncan was met by a sizeable Haggi search group, mostly on Hagg-mobiles.

They're obviously taking the search for the girls seriously.

Duncan knew a few of the Haggi but Hannibal did a full round of introductions. As well as A1/Hannibal, Sammy (B4), Punnet (B3), Lulu (A3), Sparky (A4), Steely (A2) and Strummer (D1) were present.

There was also a retired warrior, but still expert tracker, in their midst. John 'Sniffer' Dunbar was an elderly Haggi with hawk-like eyes, ridiculously bushy grey eyebrows and an aura of mischief. He carried a walking crook and had a pair of glasses resting on his nose, over a trim grey moustache.

Sniffer was clad in full plaid in a modern Dunbar Clan tartan of a deep red base with dark green squares and black and red cross threads. The plaid was accompanied with matching Hagg-boots and a Tam O'Shanter hat.

When Hannibal introduced the old tracker, Sniffer said, "Nice tae meet ye, son. Ah'm the best Haggi tracker alive, 'n' Ah'll find yir sister 'n' her pal."

Hannibal explained to Duncan and the others, "Handy 'n' Sniffer wur here early to review the car park 'n' surrounding area fur clues, initially with torches, then in the light. They've checked it o'er but Handy could'nae see any yis fir modern equipment so he went back to HHHQ 'n' left Auld Sniffer tae dae his stuff. Time's tickin' oan this search, so whit huv ye goat fir us, Sniffer?"

The old tracker had a glint in his eye, as he was given centre stage. He stated, "Wiv bin lucky thit, since the abductions, thur's nae been oany rain or much wind. Based on whit Ah've seen 'n' the clear weather, Ah've worked oot a theory."

"We trust yir instincts, Sniffer, so let's hear whit ye reckon," said Hannibal, encouraging the skilled tracker to continue.

"If ye look at the car park where the lorry wiz left, thur ur twa waiys o' gettin' in or oot. If the lorry came fae the toon main street, the wheel tracks wid show turning left 'n' then a direct line tae where the lorry is parked in the back left corner. Thir ur lots o' tracks comin' intae the car park fae that direction BUT… the tyre tracks where the lorry is parked, show thit it came in the other entrance. The lorry wiz driven at an angle across the parking area rither thun a straight line fae the other entrance. This indicates tae me, thit the lorry came in the other waiy 'n' turned RIGHT intae the car park. Therefore, it's highly likely thit it came here, fae further oot ay toon.

"We need tae yase the tyre profile 'n' try tae follae the tread, work back the waiy, along the road away fae the toon, then look fir turn marks where the lorry either enters or exits the main road. It's a long shot but it's aw wiv goat tae go oan."

Duncan and the various Haggi were staggered at the simplistic genius of Sniffer's deduction. There was no time to waste so the Haggi and Duncan checked the lorry tyre tread depth and pattern, so they would have an idea what to look for.

Hannibal instructed the group, "Pair up and go slowly along the road checking fir oany indications o' the lorry turnin'. If ye see oanythin' interestin', give me 'n' Sniffer a shout. Let's go."

As the morning progressed traffic and footfall would increase so the Haggi all travelled in sleekit mode on their Hagg-mobiles.

They took it in turns to stay out of sight or use HSW to utilise invisibility, thus conserving supply. Periodically, one of the Haggi returned to HHHQ to get fresh cans of fuel and HSW to ensure they didn't run out of either vital resource.

Duncan, meanwhile, had to make it look like he was just out for a walk, which he often did, so he didn't attract any attention.

After several hours of methodical tracking, the search group had eliminated various turnings as wild goose chases. Just as they were starting to lose faith, Punnet discovered a promising tyre tread, turning right into what looked like a farm track.

"A1, Sniffer, this looks like a possible match, huv a shuftie."

Sniffer assessed the tyre tracks, which appeared to have been in and out of this junction several times. "It's defo a possible. Let's head doon this track 'n' see whaur it taks us," he said.

Hannibal agreed and the search group were happy to get off the main drag and onto less open ground. As they walked the first few yards down the track, there was a thick line of trees all down the right-hand side, plus a four-foot-high, drystane dyke on the left. This provided loads of cover, so they all went fully visible and coasted along on their Hagg vehicles.

The tyre tread continued to show up as they progressed along the farm track and they pressed on for about half a mile. At this point, the ground rose up and the trees on the right ended, to be replaced by open fields, penned in behind a fence. In the distance they could see a set of farm buildings, including a white farm cottage, a sizeable main barn plus multiple smaller outbuildings.

No vehicles were visible.

The intrepid tracking gang were about five hundred yards away when a furtive-looking man appeared from the side door of the big, main barn. He looked up briefly then started clearing pallets and equipment from around the door area.

The search group all noticed the movement in the distance. Duncan lifted his grandad's binoculars up to his eyes and 'zoomed in' on the man. He was of average height and build, wearing dark clothes BUT… he seemed to have a mark on the left side of his face.

"Whit kin ye see?" asked Hannibal.

Duncan altered the magnification on his binoculars and there, as clear as day, was a purple birthmark. It was shaped very much like a map of Cyprus, just as Ms Robinson had told him. Duncan went into a cold sweat and adrenaline surged through his body. "I think we've found our kidnapper," he replied excitedly.

"How kin ye ken that, fae this distance?" queried Hannibal.

"He has a purple birthmark on the left side of his face. It's shaped like the map of Cyprus," Duncan responded.

"A map o' a Mediterranean island, oan ay's coupon?" said A1, incredulously.

"That's what my teacher told me about a strange guy she'd seen around. I've got a strong gut feeling that this is our guy and the girls are nearby," stated Duncan, resolutely.

"Right, let's think this through," said Hannibal, not wholly believing but starting to plan ahead.

"I'm not mucking about with the police. The girls are likely with birthmark man, let's get this done," replied Duncan, his previous hesitancy and fear consigned to the bin.

While they accepted that this could be highly dangerous or a false alarm, Duncan and the assembled Haggi formulated a quick plan of action. Duncan was not convinced the plan would work but was feeling emboldened by his previous success over the bullies and the Haggi being on hand to help.

The Haggi warriors were itching for action but respectful of Hannibal's caution and authority.

They were good to go.

Chapter 38

The search team put their plan into action. Duncan moved stealthily and steadily down the farm lane, keeping his binoculars trained on their quarry to ensure he didn't disappear from sight. As he did so, the Haggi zoomed ahead on their Hagg-mobiles in a combination of sleekit and invisible mode.

Hannibal was to act as overall coordinator. Sammy, Punnet and Steely were tasked with searching the farm premises for the girls. Old Sniffer was to act as lookout and alert the others to any danger. Sparky, Strummer and Lulu were nearby, on red alert, ready to back up Duncan on his signal.

Duncan's role was the most dangerous as he had to confront and distract the kidnapper, while appearing unthreatening. Duncan couldn't see the Haggi but kept steadily on down the farm lane, towards the farm buildings, periodically checking the man was still visible.

The Haggi reached the main barn area and stopped. They dismounted, did a quick but thorough recce to check everything was clear and no other people were on site. Satisfied that there were no others around, they carefully parked their Hagg-mobiles out of sight, behind a smaller shed.

Duncan, meanwhile, strode boldly towards the farm buildings, his heart beating like a drum. He felt anxiety at what lay ahead but was extremely determined to find Mary and Steph.

While Sniffer kept watch, Sammy and Steely went into the main barn. Punnet headed left to a smaller barn, to search there. Hannibal quickly moved round the main barn exterior and checked that the target was still outside. The man was still clearing the area around the doorway so he went into the big barn to help the others look for the captive girls.

As Hannibal went into the barn, he started to 'bubble' as his HSW was wearing off. He needed Mary to be able to see him to identify him so, rather than take another sip of HSW, he allowed himself to become visible.

After he manoeuvred past piles of farm equipment and straw bales in the barn, Hannibal saw the other two, now fully visible, Haggi. He was waved over to the far side by Steely.

Hannibal rushed across and saw that the other Haggi were standing in front of the two girls. The captive friends looked dishevelled and were blindfolded, with gags in their mouths. They were seated back to back, either side of a large, round, wooden pillar. The friends' hands were tightly bound behind their backs, with rope looped around the pillar.

To maintain Haggi secrecy, Hannibal was very mindful not to let Steph see or hear them. He gave a thumbs-up and indicated for Sammy to go and alert Duncan that they had found the girls, safe.

As Sammy quickly moved off to let Duncan know the good news, the two remaining Haggi acted in unison. Steely put his hand over Mary's mouth and Hannibal whispered very quietly in her ear, "It's yer Haggi pals come tae save ye.

Dinnae move or speak."

Mary was very startled but did as Hannibal asked.

Steely removed Mary's blindfold and had his finger over his lips indicating 'stay quiet'. He then removed the gag from her mouth and she gasped in the welcome air.

Mary was overwhelmed when she saw her two small hairy saviours in front of her and started to sob quietly in relief.

Steph heard her friend crying and said, "Mary, are you OK?"

"Yeh, I think I've just about got myself free, I'll help you in a minute," Mary lied.

Hannibal pulled his wee dirk from his Hagg-boot and cut the ropes that held Mary's feet. He then skilfully cut the rope to free her hands too, taking great care not to touch or injure Steph.

Hannibal and Steely helped Mary to her knees and she hugged them both tightly, as the relief and emotion of being free flooded through her.

Hannibal put his dirk back on his Hagg-boot, flicked open a couple of blades and handed Mary his prized Swiss Army knife. He smiled at her and indicated that she should let them get out of sight, then free Steph. He could get his knife from her later.

Mary nodded tearfully and felt a wave of fear as her Haggi heroes moved away.

Hannibal looked back, gave a thumbs-up and winked at Mary. The Haggi then disappeared around the hay bales and were gone.

Mary turned her attention to Steph. "I'm free, Steph. Stay still and quiet in case he comes back, I'm going to cut you loose."

As Mary pulled Steph's blindfold and gag free, she could see the relief in her friend's eyes. Within a couple of minutes the two friends were free and standing, hugging each other, as the blood flow resumed through their aching joints.

Steph was delighted to be free, so not remotely interested in checking the rope that had bound them. She had no idea that Mary hadn't freed herself as she had told her.

The reality of the need to leave then kicked in and the girls moved slowly and quietly towards the far door of the main barn. It took them a while to get feeling and proper movement in their legs but they were hugely relieved to no longer be bound and helpless.

Duncan, meanwhile, had got to within fifty yards of the farm building, on the blind side of the target, when the alleged kidnapper turned and made to go back inside.

"Excuse me, mister," shouted Duncan, the pitch of his voice rising nervously.

The man slowly turned to face Duncan, suspicion covering his face as this young lad had appeared from nowhere.

"What can I do for you?" asked birthmark man, trying to appear relaxed.

Sammy suddenly appeared at the barn door, behind the kidnapper, gave Duncan the thumbs-up sign and indicated they'd found the girls.

Duncan noticed the movement and subtly glanced over so as not to give any indication to the kidnapper that he was a threat, merely a primary school kid. Inwardly, he now knew this was their man but his bravado was sorely tested, as the kidnapper moved his left hand and pointed a yellow gun at him.

"Know what this is, sonny?"

Duncan just stared transfixed at the gun, speechless.

"No? Well I'll tell you what it is. This is what is commonly known as a Taser, also known as an Electronic Control Device. The police use them throughout the world as a control tool, using electric pulse shocks. This is an X26 model, which I got on the black market. It's set to Pulse Mode, full incapacity setting and can do serious short-term damage to your muscles and limbs, if I choose to fire it," he said cockily and uttered an evil laugh.

Despite feeling utter terror, Duncan replied, "I don't want any trouble, mister, I just want you to swap me for my sister, Mary. Let her go and take me in her place."

"All very noble for one so young. Been reading Shakespeare, have you?"

Duncan delayed slightly then pointed upwards to his right, the kidnapper's left, and shouted, "What the hell is that?"

As the kidnapper half turned to follow the direction, Duncan jumped backwards and to his left. The kidnapper saw nothing behind him, realised that this was a ruse, and turned back round. As he turned, the kidnapper started to press the Taser trigger, sending out a powerful electric charge.

Sparky and Lulu had reacted instantly to Duncan's warning shout.

They simultaneously yelled, "Yir gettin' dooed," and slammed into individual tackles on the back of the kidnapper's knees, just as he pressed the Taser trigger.

In a coordinated attack, Strummer sprinted forward diagonally, from behind Duncan, his wee legs going like pistons. He launched himself, like a heat-seeking missile, and delivered a crashing, flying headbutt to the kidnapper's solar plexus, knocking the wind out of him.

The crunching noise from the coordinated Haggi tackles sounded like a heavy impact Stock Car collision.

After impact, the three Haggi bounced off the kidnapper in different directions. The left-handed kidnapper folded like a jack-knifed lorry as he tried to 'zap' Duncan.

Duncan didn't feel any electric shock but the kidnapper DID, as the high voltage drilled into his OWN LEFT LEG.

The kidnapper shuddered horribly and jerked about on the ground, as if he had just been bitten by a gigantic electric eel. The Taser clattered on the ground and spun several feet away as Mary and Steph's captor fell, his limbs incapacitated by the discharge.

Once Duncan got over the shock of both the Taser shot and their crazy plan working, he checked that the kidnapper had a pulse but was completely unconscious.

He was on both counts.

Duncan said, "He's alive but totally out of it," then raced off into the farm outbuilding to find his sister.

The Haggi attackers were back on their feet and had watched, as Duncan checked the kidnapper for a pulse. They were really disappointed at not getting any follow-up action.

"Bummer thit eh's sparked oot, Ah fancied a right gid square go wi' this yin," said Strummer.

"Aye, me tae," said Lulu as she retrieved the scattered Taser.

Lulu had a mischievous look in her copper-coloured eye and toyed with the Taser as she brought it over to show Sparky.

On leaving Mary to free Steph, Hannibal sent Steely to let Punnet know the girls had been found and to then come and help the others. He then made for the open ground, outside the main barn, to check on the kidnapper, Duncan and his Haggi helpers.

As Hannibal turned the final corner Duncan, his long hair and limbs flailing, almost knocked his Haggi ally over as he rushed towards the barn.

"Sorry, Hannibal, need to see Mary, are they free?"

"Aye, is everything OK roond there?" said Hannibal, pointing in the direction of the recent Taser showdown.

"All good, got to dash."

As Duncan burst through the door of the main barn, the recently freed girls were only about twenty feet in front of him. The duo screamed loudly as the door burst open, expecting an enraged kidnapper to attack them. Instead, an out-of-breath and highly emotional Duncan came running towards them, saying, "It's all over... you're safe now... he's not going to bother you anymore."

"Holy shit, Dunc... He was crazy, armed and dangerous... How did you overpower the kidnapper?" blurted Mary.

Duncan took his time to get some breath then said calmly, "I tricked him... got him off guard and off balance... and he ended up shooting himself in the leg with the Taser... during the struggle. He's unconscious so he's no longer a threat. It's a long story, which I'll tell you later but that's the crux of it."

Steph said, "Wow, you're a hero and you saved us," as the three of them went into a bizarre, manic, circular hug of celebration.

As Duncan, his sister and her bestie were enjoying their emotional reunion nearby, the Haggi were in 'clear-up' mode. The warriors, using available binding materials, had trussed up the kidnapper like a pig on a spit. He wouldn't be able to move, even if he did regain consciousness.

The Haggi had all been accounted for, they'd done a quick sense check and clear up, then Hannibal had signalled a swift exit.

We need to be out of sight before Steph appears.

All bar one of them took a good gulp of HSW, turned invisible and mounted up on their Hagg-mobiles to head off back to HHHQ.

A distant puttering sound could be heard as they started to move away.

The niggling impatience from earlier finally got the better of Lulu and just before the Haggi headed off, she unloaded another Taser blast into the kidnapper. "Jist tae mak shair eh disnae gie Dunc oany mair trouble," she said to justify her action.

Lulu then zoomed off on her Hagg-mobile but unlike the others, she'd forgotten to take a drink of HSW or adopt sleekit mode on her vehicle.

The freed girls and Duncan made their way into the open air. The girls had to shield their eyes for some time to adjust to the bright daylight so Steph didn't see Lulu's Hagg-mobile zooming off. She did, however, hear the roar of Lulu's revving engine.

"What's that revving engine noise?" asked Steph curiously.

"I didn't heard anything, Mary. Did you?" replied Duncan, staring intently at his sister to back him up.

"No, I didn't hear anything. Maybe a farm vehicle, Steph?" Mary replied rhetorically.

The siblings avoided eye contact, as they knew the truth about the Haggi involvement. They were also both massively grateful for the Haggi being true to their word and helping

Clan McPherson avoid possible disaster.

Duncan and Mary didn't realise but Hannibal was only a few yards away, invisible but still watching over them.

I'd best hing aroond tae mak sair thir awright.

Chapter 39

As the three youngsters moved across the farmyard area, the girls' eyes fully adjusted to the daylight. The earlier puttering sound had grown substantially in volume and a green, mud-spattered tractor pulling a flatbed trailer, drove up to them. A huge, jolly, round-faced farmer stopped the tractor, switched it off and jumped down to the ground.

"What's been going on here? I was going down the lane there and must have been downwind, as I heard shouting, a strange buzzing sound and what sounded like a fight. Is everything OK?"

Duncan introduced himself and the girls to the farmer then pointed to the trussed up kidnapper and provided a loose outline of what had happened. No mention of any external help was made.

"Oh my god, I heard about this kidnapping – terrible business. Your parents will be frantic to know your safe. Let's just get you all to town on the tractor and trailer. It'll be just as quick as driving back to my farm to phone from the landline. I don't believe in these modern fangled mobiles," said the farmer.

Duncan was so high on adrenaline that he completely

forgot he had his mobile in his pocket. The girls' phones had been confiscated by the kidnapper and were still in the farm cottage.

By the time the farmer and Duncan started to lift the kidnapper onto the trailer, Hannibal was making dust on his Hagg-mobile in 'sleekit mode.' He made quick time to the house of Davy Smith, Duncan's best pal.

As Davy was already aware of the Haggi, Hannibal knew he could be trusted. He briefly explained what had happened and asked Davy to go quickly to the parents at the Findlay house. His instruction was to tell the two sets of parents that he'd heard that there had been developments and the girls had been found, SAFE AND WELL. They needed to go to the police incident room in town as soon as possible.

Davy was a bit bemused by Hannibal's request but quickly made his way to the Findlay house as requested. He knew the property but had never been to the house before.

The size of the house and grounds was quite impressive as Davy made his way to the front door and rang the bell.

Bryan Findlay, Steph's ex-footballer dad, opened the door and wondered who this young lad was. Davy nervously explained that he had important news and was ushered into the kitchen, where all the parents were.

Cath said, "Davy, why are you here? Have you heard something?"

"Yes, I heard the girls are safe, you need to get to the police station as soon as possible."

The adults didn't see fit to ask any follow-up questions but just went into autopilot. Davy was almost run over in the prevailing whirlwind of parents scrambling for the door.

He just about got out the front door before Bryan Findlay

slammed it shut and locked it.

George McPherson had already started up his Lexus as Bryan jumped in, joining the other three frantic parents. The engine growled and the tyres squealed as George gunned it heading for the police station. He drove like a man possessed and, in what seemed like a blink of an eye, brought the car to a screeching halt, right beside the police incident HQ.

Cath was inside the portacabin and demanding information before George was even out of the car. "What's happened to the girls? Where are they?" she asked breathlessly, of the officer in front of her.

"We don't have anything of note to update you with, Mrs McPherson, I'm sorry," said the police officer, apologetically.

"There must be some horrible mistake. We were told there was news… and they were OK…" blurted Cath before dissolving in a pool of tears, her nerves shredded.

"We'll let you know as soon as we have any further news," added the police officer, awkwardly.

Maggie Findlay comforted Cath as the four parents came to terms with their misinformation.

After five or six minutes of heartbreaking nothingness, George urged them all back to the car to return to the Findlay home. They made their way out, despondently, to the abandoned Lexus and George used the remote to unlock the doors. Cath was just about to climb into the back seat when she heard a *putt, putt, putt* type noise and a tractor and trailer came slowly into view heading towards them.

Cath thought her heart was going to burst when she saw Mary and Steph's heads appear above the top of the tractor cabin, as they stood up on the trailer.

The farmer braked and stopped.

The two kidnapped friends shrieked loudly, as they leapt down and ran into their respective mothers' arms, crying tears of joy. Parents and daughters alike gathered in a big emotional embrace.

Even George was getting tearful.

The farmer restarted the tractor and edged forward.

Davy had just run into view and could scarcely believe what he saw as the tractor turned side on. There was Dunc sitting on top of the unconscious and heavily bound kidnapper.

Others soon started to realise this too. Several police officers spilled out of the station and incident cabin to check what all the commotion was. Duncan and the farmer gave the police an outline explanation and the girls confirmed that the unconscious man was their abductor. The kidnapper was taken away to hospital for checking over then interviewed under police caution.

The joyous parents took their children home, enormously relieved that things had turned out as they had.

Chapter 40

After the dust settled and investigations had been carried out, the police issued a statement. This confirmed that a fifty-six-year-old man named Melvin McMurdo was in custody and would be charged with stalking, kidnapping and illegal possession and use of a Taser. They commended Duncan McPherson, the younger brother of one of the kidnapped girls, for his outstanding bravery and actions in saving his sister Mary and her best friend Steph Findlay from their ordeal.

It was later revealed that the kidnapper was a disgruntled ex-teacher, sacked from Auchterbarn Secondary School a decade before for gross misconduct (inappropriate behaviour towards female pupils). Mr McMurdo wasn't charged at that time but was warned off and asked to leave the area. As a result he was shunned by his family and peers so had moved away under a cloud.

He had found work elsewhere and stayed away for several years but then felt the urge to return and seek revenge at the school he formerly taught at. He had stalked the victims then sought revenge and money through the kidnap plot.

The police had interviewed the victims, the perpetrator and Duncan, plus the farmer to try to ascertain exactly what had happened and prepare a case for court.

When it came to Duncan's interview he had stuck to the basics, namely:-

- He wanted to do something to help rather than sitting around.
- He had been out looking for the girls and saw the man on the farm.
- It didn't feel right so he used his binoculars to zoom in and ID'd the birthmark, which his teacher had told him about.
- Went to investigate.
- Kidnapper pulled a Taser gun and graphically explained how it worked.
- He was only a young lad and unarmed so the only thing he could think of was to offer to swap himself for Mary.
- Tricked the kidnapper to look away momentarily then got him off balance and into a struggle.
- Taser went off.
- Kidnapper shot himself by accident and was unconscious.
- Found the girls in the barn after they had freed themselves.
- Farmer helped to tie the kidnapper up and throw him on the trailer.
- The farmer didn't have a mobile and felt it would be quicker just to drive to town rather than go back to farm house and call the police.
- Delivered the kidnapper to police on the trailer.

The Scene of Crime evidence somewhat backed up the Taser-firing elements but, otherwise, there were considerable inconsistencies. In all the other witness statements, the only hints towards involvement of other parties were the farmer's mention of hearing strong Scottish accents, which didn't sound like Duncan, and inconsistencies in who freed who, and when. In addition, the farmer had no recall of helping to tie the kidnapper up.

Steph's mysterious 'motorbike-like' noise just after they were rescued was never adequately explained but put down as the tractor approaching.

Duncan and Mary never mentioned anything about the wee hairy Haggi that had helped to save the day. This would continue to remain their secret.

The police were a long way from convinced that Duncan could overpower the kidnapper by himself and then apply mega-strength, complex knots to tie him up, even with help. However, they had a great result handed to them on a plate so hadn't looked too hard for any other explanation.

In the aftermath, Duncan tried to play down his role behind closed doors and hint at help from his new friends.

Cath dismissed these claims as nonsense. She was just delighted that her daughter was OK and she lavished praise on Duncan, her new hero.

Mary never let on but was going through some major turmoil of her own, dealing with the events of the last few weeks.

The media reporting of the kidnap went viral in no time. It was huge locally but also across Scotland, the wider UK and eventually worldwide. The Haggeroos in Australia saw the coverage, as did the Haggaleros in Spain and Mexico. Duncan McPherson's actions were known across the globe, the twisted kidnapper was in custody, the girls were safe and remarkably he was a worldwide HERO.

Up in HHHQ the Senior Council had been informed of the successful rescue of the kidnapped girls. In recognition of such a happy outcome and a successful Haggi mission, they made a special order. Mental Mac was requested to open the Berry Brew vaults, so that the Haggi could celebrate in proper style.

Epilogue

It was Thursday, in the first full week of the new school year. The crazy events of the recent summer holidays were starting to fade from the memory of those not directly impacted.

Jimmy Brown, AKA Superman the lorry float driver, had eventually been found in his shed and freed by a concerned neighbour. He was extremely dehydrated and hungry but recovered with no ill-effects. Jimmy was hugely embarrassed by being duped by the kidnapper and decided not to drive in the parade again.

The farmer and his wife, from the kidnap farm premises, had been found by the police, bound and gagged in their farmhouse cottage, soon after the kidnapper was handed over. They were not injured but were undergoing trauma counselling.

Murdo the kidnapper was remanded in prison custody, awaiting trial. He was full of remorse for his actions, had cooperated with the police, and it was hoped that he would plead guilty, to avoid putting the victims and families through a trial.

George had resumed work and life with Marlene, without

so much as a backwards glance. His ransom money was still safely in the bank and he had not taken his kids out since the kidnapping episode or checked on their wellbeing.

Cath was simply relieved and content that her kids were both unscathed, at least physically, from the kidnap episode. Work in the medical practice was back to its familiar flow and she had met a guy at her dance class. His request for a date was still being considered!

Mary had been reunited with her iPhone after it was recovered from the farm cottage and checked over by the police. The phone continued to be an extension of her right arm. She still had a fair way to go to resume 'normality' but her flashbacks and nightmares had stopped, after undergoing several counselling sessions on the back of her kidnap ordeal.

Hannibal and Lulu had visited her one day, while her mum was out, to provide a pep talk. Mary appreciated their visit, enjoyed their company and had handed back Hannibal's treasured Swiss Army knife.

Mary had tentatively returned to second year at secondary school. She was being given plenty of comfort and support from fellow kidnap victim Steph and the wider Glam Gang, none of whom had any inkling of the existence of the Haggi.

Boyfriends were very much on the back burner for Mary.

Talking of which, Brad Thomas!

After the Haggi video revelations, he moved to the North of Scotland. Brad continues to lure women into his web but now his focus is on more mature ladies rather than inexperienced teenagers. His primary aim nowadays, is to bag a place to live for a short while, then move on before he is rumbled and while his looks still have value.

Duncan's world was hugely transformed. He and Davy no

longer looked for the safety of the shadows at school, as the Burgan boys were no longer a threat. The former twin bullies were now first years at the secondary school but merely timid minnows in a very big pond.

Further to his heroics in the kidnap and the follow-up media coverage, other pupils now respected and actively engaged with Duncan. Rumours abounded locally that he had access to special powers and after his victories over the bullies and the kidnapper, he was someone to be admired and not taken lightly.

For all his newfound celebrity, Duncan himself was still most at ease doing what he'd always done. When not at school, he spent most of his time doing his art, being close to nature (often with Davy in tow) and keeping out of the way of people when he could. His big sister gave him much less of a hard time than previously, as she knew, first hand, how much he really cared for and looked out for her.

The lovely Jenny Paterson now spoke to Duncan occasionally, around town, but was still a distance jewel, although he felt confident he could win her over in time.

The primary school had one major change in that Ms Robinson's idea for the Sunshine Seat had been implemented by the head teacher. The shiny, new, yellow bench shone resplendently in the late summer light, a beacon to those in need of some brightness.

Rowena Robinson herself looked trimmer than a few months before. She had trendy highlights in her hair and wore new, colourful, well-fitted clothes, as a personal reward for her five months sober milestone.

It was halfway through the lunch break as Ms Robinson looked out on the Sunshine Seat from the top floor staff room in Auchterbarn Primary School. She smiled inwardly and thought, *Teaching WILL be REWARDING this year.*

As Ms Robinson turned away from the staff room window, a forlorn-looking figure made his way to the Sunshine Seat and slowly slumped down. His name was Daniel Addison, a new arrival in Auchterbarn, starting out in primary five. Although he'd eaten a decent lunch, his stomach lurched with sadness as he stared at the ground between his shaking knees. He was a quiet, only child, very much the new kid in town, had no pals yet and wasn't confident enough to try to make some.

Daniel lifted his head as he heard someone approaching the Sunshine Seat. A tall, gangly boy sat down beside him and said, encouragingly, "Hi, I'm Duncan. I know things can be hard but I'm here to help make things better. Now, why don't you tell me what's going on? A problem shared, is a problem halved."

A ray of hope flickered across Daniel's face, as he started to tell this nice lad his story and fears.

Maybe things are going to be alright.

By the time the bell rang to start the afternoon lessons, Daniel Addison was walking across the playground, chatting and laughing, with two primary five classmates. Duncan had briefly introduced them, then left them to it.

As Duncan watched the primary fives from a distance, the clear voice of Grandad Hamish, whispered in his ear, "I'm very proud of you, son."

Duncan smiled as he crossed the playground and was last to go back in. He stepped into the main corridor, closed the door and disappeared from outside view.

Davy watched from further along the corridor and admired his friend, hoping that one day he'd be bold enough to tell him how he truly felt about him.

Sitting, camouflaged in a nearby tree, Hannibal had a wee tear in his eye as he marvelled at the personal growth and newfound maturity of Duncan, his friend and the newest Haggi Connector.

The End

Jockanese Translator

Note – many Jockanese words miss off the 'g' in a word ending in -ing. E.g. laughin' = laughing.

Aboot – about
Aff – off
Ah – I
Ah'm – I'm
Ain – own
Airm – arm
Alki – an alcoholic or a person who drinks to excess and/or has a drink problem
Aroond – around
Aw – all
Awright – alright
Awthin' – everything
Ay – of
Ay'ways – always
Baith – both
Banjoed – walloped, hit hard (as if by a swinging banjo)
Banter – social interplay
Bawbag – a derogatory term for a lowlife or bad person
Bein' – being
Belter – excellent/cracking example
Bide – stay, remain, live

Bit – North East term for a boot (footwear)
Bitter – Better (a more northern pronunciation)
Biz – either a colloquial shortened version of Bisset surname OR business – as in 'just the biz' (business)/liking good/hits the mark
Boak – sick, vomit (noun and/or verb)
Braw – lovely, very good
Bud – friendly term similar to friend, pal, mate
Bummer – a downer or let-down
Bunnet – a Scottish woollen flat cap
Burn – stream, small river
Cairry – carry
Cairrier – carrier
Cannae – can't
Caw – call
Cheeky git – chancing chap
Come fi' – come from
Comfy – comfortable
Coo – cow
Cooncil – council
Coz – because
Coupon – face
Cried – named, called
Da' – dad
Dae – do
Daein' – doing
Digs – living accommodation
Dinnae – don't
Dirk – dagger, knife
Disnae – doesn't
Doo – a pigeon OR to batter someone in a fight

Doon – down
Dunt – hit
Dyke – wall
Eftir – after
Eh – he
Eh's – his
Erse – arse, bum, backside
Fae or Frae – from
Faimily – family
Fecht – fight
Fiert/feard – frightened
Fir or Fur – for
Fit – North East Scotland usage – can mean what, foot or which, depending on context.
E.g. **Fit Fit** – means 'which foot'!!
Fit Like – North East colloquial term for 'How's it going?'
Flair – floor
Follae – follow
Foo – full
Foostie – derogatory term for someone or something, literally means smelling of mould
Gairden – garden
Gie – give
Giein' – giving
Gid – good
Gie – give
Git – get – also used as a mildly derogatory term, similar to devil, 'ya sly git' (you sly devil)
Goat – got – also standard English for a farm animal
Gonnae – going to
Greet – cry

Greetin' – crying
Grund – ground
Gutty – gusto, effort
Hame – home
Hank Marvin – starvin' (starving), rhyming slang
Haud – hold
Heid – head
Hen – an affectionate term for a girl or woman. E.g. Morning hen = Morning dear.
Hing – hang
Hirsute – Latin-derived word meaning hairy
Himsel or Hissel – himself
Honkin' – foul smelling
Hoose – house
How's it hingin'? – Colloquial phrase meaning, 'How are you?'
Howsat – how is that?
Humpty – unjustifiably grumpy or moody
Huv – have
Huvin' – having
Huvin' a giraffe – rhyming slang for 'having a laugh' (a term of disbelief)
Huvty – have to
Huz – has
'Il – will
Intae or in tae – into or in to
Jaiket – jacket
Jist – just
Joab – job
Jobbie – a turd, shit, excrement
Ken – know
Kent – known

Kickin' – a thumping or physical assault
Kin – can
Knittin' – knitting
Knottin' – doubled over in laughter
Laddie – boy
Laldy – big effort, all you've got
Lassie – girl
Loadsae – lots of
Lugs – ears
Luvin – loving
Ma – my
Mair – more
Mak – make
Masel – myself
Maw – mother
Minger – a smelly person
Moby – mobile phone
Muckle – big, huge
'n' – and
Nae – no
Nivir – never
Noo – now
Nowt – nothing
O' – of
O'er – over
Oan – on
Oany – any
Oanythin' – anything
Oner – in one attempt
Oorsels – ourselves, us
Oot – out

Ootstandin' – outstanding
Ower – over
Passin' – passing
Pillae – pillow
Pittin' – putting
Plaid – a long piece of tartan material, worn over the shoulder as part of Scottish Highland dress
Plums – testicles, male genitals
Pong – smell
Probs – problem(s)
Puke – vomit/sick
Punnet – a small box or basket for storing fruit or veg in (e.g. a punnet of strawberries)
Radge – a nutcase or daft person, often used as a term of endearment
Reckin – reckon
Richt – right
Rip ma knittin' – wind me up/annoy me – *literally: tear down my (existing) knitting*
Rithir – rather
Roond – round
Roosed – fired up, motivated
Sair – sore
Sannies – sandwiches
Scratcher – one's bed
Scrote – derogatory term for a lowlife
Scunnered – hacked off, upset, disheartened, seriously miffed
Sec – a second
Shair – sure
Shift yer erse – get moving, get your butt in gear
Shuftie – look

Skelp – hit
Skiver – a work dodger
Smidge – smidgeon, a little bit
Sporran – a small, purse like, pouch that hangs around the waist as part of male Scottish Highland dress
Square go – a fight
Squeeze Box – (accordion, musical instrument)
Stane – stone
Swattin' – swatting, studying up on
Tabs – tablets
Tae – usually means 'to' but occasionally means 'toe', as in: sair tae (sore toe)
Taes – toes
Tak – take
Telt – told
Thae – those
The day – today (Haggi tend to say 'the day' rather than 'today')
The morra – tomorrow
The night – tonight
Thin – than
Thir – their
Thit – that
Tho' – though
Thon – that
Thum – them
Thun – than
Thur – their
Timin'll – timing will
Toon – town
Toppin' – topping
Trotters – feet

Tube – an idiot
Twa or Twae – two
Um – him
Uncomfy – uncomfortable
Ur – are
Waiy – way
Wee – small
Weel – well
Weel-fired rolls – white bread rolls with a burnt top
Whae – who
Whae's – who is
Whaur – where
Whey – who
Whit – what
Whit's – what is
Wi' – with
Windae – window
Withoot – without
Wir/Wur – generally means were or we're; note that wur can also mean our
Wiz – was
Wurries – worries
Ya – you – e.g. 'ya chancer'
Yase(d) – use(d) as in utilise
Ye – you
Yer – you are OR your
Yid – you had
Yil – you will
Yin – one
Yir – your
Yirsel – yourself

Yirsels – yourselves
Yis – use (as in 'no use') – 'it's nae yis tae me' = 'it's of no use to me'.
Yiv – you have
Youse – you (plural)

ACKNOWLEDGEMENTS

A big thank you to all my family, friends and contacts for getting me to this stage and the book into print. Especially, Jane, my wonderful wife who indulges my 'crazy brain' and puts up with me getting up during the night to scribble down script ideas.

ABOUT THE AUTHOR

Stephen is in his late fifties and retired from financial services.

He lives in Edinburgh with his wife Jane and is a big sports fan, especially football, golf, baseball and cricket.

He remains a plus handicap golfer even at his advanced age and has won National championships and represented Scotland in amateur golf at schools, boys, youths and full international level as well as captaining Great Britain and Ireland Youths.

Writing of a novel is a new pursuit but he has always been an avid reader and has previously written poems and one, (unpublished) short story.

Printed in Great Britain
by Amazon